THE INN AT WILLA BAY

A WILLA BAY NOVEL

NICOLE ELLIS

LEAPING RABBIT PRESS

1

Zoe

"What do you think about having the actual wedding ceremony over there, under the pergola?" Zoe Tisdale pointed to the far end of the garden where a white wooden arch framed a million-dollar view of Willa Bay's deep blue waters. "It's our most popular choice for ceremonies, but I can show you a few other locations around the grounds if you're interested in something different."

"It's gorgeous," the bride-to-be said breathily as she spun around in slow circles. "This is like being in a secret garden. Can I take a closer look at the arch?"

Zoe smiled at her. New clients were always impressed when they saw the gardens at Willa Bay Lodge. "Of course. Let me know what you think. I want to make sure everything about this wedding is exactly what you were hoping for."

While the other woman crossed the expansive lawn to

check out the pergola and its adjacent gardens, Zoe took the opportunity to relax a little and enjoy her surroundings. Typical for April in the Pacific Northwest, it had rained that morning, but the clouds had burned off by the afternoon, just in time for Zoe to show her client around. Japanese maples, azaleas, and boxwoods formed a border around the Pergola Garden, the largest outdoor space on the grounds. White wrought-iron benches, dispersed randomly in almost-hidden alcoves off the main lawn, peeked out like treasures waiting for guests to discover them.

To keep the landscaping pristine, the grounds crew would be outside soon to towel off the benches and rake up any leaves that had fallen during the storm. The fragrance of roses hung in the air, mixing with the scent of recent rain and a hint of salt from the bay. If Zoe wasn't on the clock, she would have loved nothing more than to grab a book from the Lodge's library and sneak away to a dry seat overlooking the water.

"I love it," the woman said from behind her, breaking Zoe out of her reverie. "How many people did you say this area can accommodate?"

"About two hundred seated." Zoe gestured to the lawn in front of the pergola. "For weddings, we usually have two sections of rows with an aisle down the middle. If there's a chance of rain, we have a canopy that's large enough to shelter the whole garden." She stared up at the gray clouds that threatened to obscure the sun, then gave the woman a wry grin. "The weather in August should be fine, but you never know in Washington. We like to be prepared for anything."

The woman nodded, bouncing lightly on the balls of her feet. "It's exactly what we've been looking for. I can't wait until my fiancé sees this." She was so giddy that she looked like she might start jumping with glee – something Zoe had actually seen brides do when they locked down their wedding venue.

"I'm so glad you like it. Let's go inside, and we can start working on a plan." Zoe motioned to the woman to follow her back into the Lodge.

In Zoe's office, they discussed most of the major details of the event, including flowers, catering choices, the cake, and music. While the Lodge had its own dining room for guests, it offered clients the option to bring in outside caterers for larger events. Zoe made a note to follow up with her client in another month to check on her progress and see if she needed any other assistance. Although it technically wasn't in her job description to help clients with all of their wedding details, Zoe had worked as an event coordinator at the Lodge for over nine years, and she'd found that going the extra mile to make sure things were on track early in the process was key to a successful event.

After the woman left, Zoe went into her boss's office. Joan was seated behind her desk, her reading glasses perched on the edge of her nose as she peered at her computer screen.

She looked up when Zoe entered. "Hey. How did your client intake go this afternoon? Did it ever stop raining so you could show her the gardens?" Joan glanced at the windowless walls of her office with distaste. "I feel like I'm locked in a pit in here. It could be midnight for all I know." Her eyes widened, and she removed her reading glasses. "It's not, is it?"

Zoe laughed. "It's only four-thirty in the afternoon, but it sounds like you need to take a break. Or maybe head home for the day." Joan put in just as many hours as Zoe did, if not more, so it didn't surprise Zoe that Joan had lost track of time.

Joan shook her head. "Too much to do before I knock off for the day. I could use a cup of coffee though." She rolled her ergonomic chair backward and stood, resting her hands on the desk for balance. "I'm getting too old for this."

"Only three more weeks." Zoe moved into the hallway to allow Joan room to exit the office, then walked with her to the kitchen. "Are you getting excited?"

Joan shrugged. "Yes and no. I've been doing this for so long that it's hard to imagine being retired. Not that we'll be lazy in our retirement though. Fred has the next few years planned out for us: A trip to Italy, a cruise to Hawaii, and, of course, traveling to see all the kids and their families." A wistful expression came over her face. "I *am* looking forward to seeing my grandbabies more often."

Zoe edged open the door to the kitchen, taking care to make sure there wasn't anyone on the other side. They walked over to the counter where the chef, Taylor, always had a pot of coffee going for the staff. Joan filled two mugs, handing one to Zoe before leaning against the counter to drink her own.

"How's it going?" a dark-haired woman in her early thirties asked as she stepped out of the walk-in refrigerator with an armload of fresh vegetables.

"Hey, Meg," Zoe said. "Things are going pretty good. I think Joan and I finally got all of the details sorted out for the wedding this Saturday."

Meg Briggs scowled. "I heard things were going haywire with that wedding. I know Taylor is up in arms about all the menu changes. I could have sworn he was going to cancel the event after the seventh time the bride changed her mind about the entrée choices." She set bags of potatoes and onions on the counter, then neatly stacked whole carrots in a pile, their feathery green fronds hanging over the edge like moss from a tree.

"I think we got it all straightened out." Joan set her cup on the counter and sighed. "I'm definitely not going to miss dealing with all of the crazy client requests." She nodded to Zoe. "That's going to be up to you and whoever George hires to take your place."

"I'm glad I don't have to deal with most of the guests in person." Meg turned to Zoe, and her voice dropped to a whisper. "Has George said anything about you taking over?"

Zoe shook her head. "No, but he's not always the most organized person in the world. I wouldn't be surprised if he offers me the job the day after Joan leaves." She grimaced. "Or maybe he doesn't think I'm the right person for the position."

She sipped the strong coffee to distract herself, but truth be told, she *was* getting a little worried. Joan had announced her retirement plans over a month ago, and although George had made comments indicating he'd be promoting Zoe, he hadn't said it outright.

"Are you kidding me?" Meg shot her an incredulous look. "Who else would he hire?"

"Don't be ridiculous, honey. You're a shoo-in to be my replacement – everyone knows it." Joan picked up her coffee mug from the counter. "Speaking of work, though, I need to get back to my desk if I want any chance of being home for dinner with Fred tonight."

"I'm going to finish my coffee and head home," Zoe said. "I came in at the crack of dawn this morning to work on a client proposal, and now I'm beat."

"See you in the morning." Joan left the kitchen,

sipping her coffee as she walked out the door.

"Are you sure you want Joan's job?" Meg eyed the closed door. "She must put in at least sixty hours a week."

Zoe smiled. "More like eighty hours during the summer. But yes, I've always dreamed of being the event manager at a place like this. Even when I was a little kid, I was staging weddings for my Barbie and Ken dolls. I just love seeing the joy on people's faces at an event I helped organize."

She'd been working at the Lodge as an event coordinator since graduating from college and had always hoped to move up the ranks when Joan retired. Over the years, Willa Bay had become her home, and she wanted to stay there long-term, but unfortunately, even in the wedding capital of the Pacific Northwest, there wasn't much room for advancement in the industry. If this didn't work out, she wasn't sure what her future held.

"Well, stop worrying about it." Meg gave her a quick hug. "I've got to get things prepped for the dinner rush before Taylor comes back. I'm off tomorrow and Thursday, but I'll see you at the Wedding Crashers meeting, okay?"

"Sounds good." Zoe gulped the last of her lukewarm coffee and placed the cup in the commercial dishwasher. "Is your mom coming to the meeting on Friday?"

A shadow crossed Meg's face. "I think so. She has her one-year cancer checkup that day and a scan, so it depends on how she's feeling."

Zoe nodded. When Debbie Briggs was diagnosed with breast cancer two years ago, Meg had been working as a sous-chef in Portland, Oregon. Being hundreds of miles away while her mom underwent chemotherapy treatments had been stressful, and Meg had eventually moved back home to Willa Bay to be closer to her family.

Debbie had been cancer-free for a year now, but Zoe knew it was something that was always on her friend's mind.

Zoe squeezed Meg's arm reassuringly. "She's going to be fine."

Meg pressed her lips together, then nodded. "I know. But I'll feel better when the scan tells me that too." She picked up a chef's knife and expertly diced a carrot, sliding it to the corner of her cutting board before starting on the next one.

Zoe took that as her cue to leave. She exited the kitchen, ducking into her office to grab her purse and lightweight rain jacket. When she came back out into the hallway, she stopped short. The Lodge's owner, George, was standing in front of his office, chatting with an unfamiliar man wearing a preppy polo shirt and khaki pants. She started to greet George, but he averted his gaze and hurriedly ushered the man into his office.

Her blood ran cold. What was going on? George was never overly friendly, but he was usually cordial and professional, so this was out of character for him. Who was his mystery guest? She knew she was probably being paranoid, but she couldn't help but wonder if he was interviewing someone for Joan's job. Event manager was a key position at the Lodge and carried with it a great deal of responsibility. Did he not think she was up to it?

Her grandfather often said worrying didn't solve anything, and he was right. She forced herself to head outside to her car, taking deep breaths of the salt- and floral-scented air. By the time she'd pulled out of the staff parking lot and onto the main road leading into town, she was feeling better.

The town of Willa Bay was located about an hour north of Seattle, hugging the coastline for a few miles before the road turned inland. Most of the commercial area centered on Main Street bordered by the Willomish River before it flowed into the bay. It had once been a planned resort community for Seattleites before air travel became a popular mode of transportation. Zoe passed by the entrance to Main Street and drove over the red bridge that linked the northern and southern sections of town. Although most of Willa Bay was within walking distance, the cottage she rented was on the far side of town from the Lodge, so she preferred to drive to work to save time.

About a mile from the bridge, she turned down a gravel road to get to the old Inn at Willa Bay. A canopy of trees cast shadows across the driveway, making it difficult to maneuver around the deep potholes pocking the surface. As much as she loved her landlord, property maintenance wasn't Celia's strong suit.

She parked in front of her cottage which was one of twenty guest houses on the property, most with stunning views of the water. When she'd moved in, she'd painted hers a light turquoise, giving it a cheery appearance that set it off from the rest. Once upon a time, the others had also sported charming pastel hues, but now their siding was faded and rotting in places. It saddened her to compare the cottages' current appearance to how they must have looked when the resort was in its heyday.

At least she'd been able to save one of them, and it had been a lifesaver for her. Real estate in Willa Bay wasn't cheap, and she'd struggled to find an affordable place to live when she'd taken the job at the Lodge. Finding this place had been a stroke of luck, and she was thankful every day for her good fortune.

She unlocked the door and tossed her purse and

jacket on the sofa under the front window before going into the bedroom to change out of her work clothes. She dressed quickly in a comfortable pair of jeans she'd had since high school and a long-sleeved T-shirt, then went out the front door, shutting it tightly behind her without locking it. Around here, raccoons were a bigger problem than burglars so she rarely locked it unless she'd be gone all day.

The driveway continued on past the other cottages, but she walked in the opposite direction, following a well-worn path that wound through a thicket of blackberry bushes. Soon, the dirt under her feet turned to sand. The tide was out, exposing barnacle-covered rocks and beds of kelp and seaweed that clung to thick mounds of pebbles. Unlike the sandy ocean beaches she'd grown up with, the terrain here was much rockier and sloped down sharply at one point, revealing a drop-off that would surprise anyone wading in the water after the tide came in.

A dark cloud hung over Whidbey Island, depositing a sheet of silvery rain on the other side of the bay. She stopped in front of a beach log and sat down on the sand, hugging her knees up to her chest. It may have been sunny, but a stiff breeze blew off the water, making her wish she'd brought her jacket.

She always came to the beach when she needed to think. Besides Willa Bay being the self-proclaimed "Wedding Capital of the Pacific Northwest," its proximity to the water had been a big draw when she was deciding where to live after graduation. She'd grown up in Haven Shores, a small Washington town located on the Pacific Ocean, hours away from Willa Bay. Pops, her grandfather, still lived there, and her brother, Luke, had settled in the neighboring town of Candle Beach.

She stared at the surf. The waves in Willa Bay were different from back home – smaller, but just as mesmerizing as the giant ocean waves she was used to. She blinked back tears. Work at the Lodge had been crazy-busy lately, and it had been too long since she'd last seen Pops and Luke. Thank goodness she'd be going home in a few weeks to celebrate Pops's eighty-fifth birthday.

That thought raised Zoe's spirits, and she tore her gaze away from the water, her eyes landing on the aging gazebo near the main structure on the property. She loved how the gazebo stood guard above the beach. Secretly, she'd dreamed of what it would be like to be married there, practically standing on the beach as she recited her vows. Not that such a thing was likely to come to pass.

She'd had a handful of relationships over the years, but they hadn't progressed much beyond a few dates. The men she'd gone out with hadn't liked the hours she devoted to work, so she'd long ago decided that a serious relationship wasn't in the cards for her. Once she took over Joan's job, the hours would be even longer. Zoe was up for the challenge, but she wondered if she'd ever regret giving up so much for her career.

She eyed the gazebo's sagging roofline and sighed. It was more likely to fall into the bay than ever bear witness to her wedding.

The ominous gray cloud she'd seen earlier had edged closer to the mainland, and a fat raindrop plopped down on her head as a warning, followed immediately by dozens more. She leapt to her feet and jogged back to the trail leading to her cottage as tiny wet bombs pelted her in quick succession. When she reached the shelter of the trees, she slowed to a walk to enjoy the stillness. The pine needles underfoot cushioned her feet with every step, and the air held the tang of rain, much like it had earlier in the Pergola Garden.

Zoe's thoughts cleared as she approached her cottage. Tomorrow, she'd ask George about the promotion. Once things were settled with that, she'd feel a lot better.

2

CASSIE

Cassie Thorsen reread the email from her son Jace's third-grade teacher, then pushed back her chair and stood from the small desk she'd set up in one corner of her kitchen. She paced the short distance between the sliding glass door leading to the backyard and the entrance to the living room, pulling her long blonde hair back into a ponytail as she walked.

This wasn't the first time his teacher had warned her that he wasn't doing well with transitions between classes at school. This time, he'd refused to leave the classroom for lunch until he'd completed the math problems they'd been working on. Cassie had tried talking to him about similar issues in the past, but he'd insisted that he couldn't stop until a task was finished.

His doctor had diagnosed him with ADHD – Attention Deficit Hyperactivity Disorder – but Jace's problems seemed to extend beyond the hallmarks of that diagnosis. His doctor had recommended that he be formally assessed for autism, but they'd been waiting for over a year for an evaluation at the Seattle Autism Center.

Cassie looked over at the Disney wall calendar hanging above her desk. Now that the appointment was only a few days away, she wasn't sure how she felt. Part of her hoped the assessment would provide some answers, but another part of her feared the finality of a diagnosis, one way or the other.

High-pitched laughter rang out from the direction of the front yard, followed by the shriek of the ungreased hinges of the door as it swung open. The kids were home from school. She walked into the living room, where Jace had already engrossed himself in a complicated Lego build at the table she'd set up for him against the wall.

"Where's Amanda?" she asked.

He didn't respond, so Cassie opened the front door again, grimacing at how loud it had become. She'd done her best to keep up on home repairs since her divorce had been finalized two years ago, but with two kids, a full-time job as the pastry chef at the Willa Bay Lodge, and a cake decorating business on the side, little annoyances like a squeaky door hadn't been a priority.

Outside, her ten-year-old daughter, Amanda, stood at the curb with her best friend, Cammie, who lived next door. Amanda waved her hands through the air, gesticulating rapidly while wearing a broad smile on her face.

Cassie grinned and shook her head. Looks-wise, Amanda took after her father, with wavy dark hair and chocolate-brown eyes. However, she was as much of a social butterfly as Cassie herself had been at that age, a trait that made relating to Jace's natural introversion difficult for both of them.

"Amanda, it's time to do your homework," Cassie called out.

"I don't have that much tonight," Amanda said. "Can I go over to Cammie's house for a while?"

Cassie glanced at the house next door. Usually, she was fine with Amanda going over to Cammie's house after school because she knew her daughter would breeze through her homework before bedtime. Today, however, it was her ex-husband Kyle's weekend with the kids, and he'd be over to pick them up in less than two hours.

She shook her head. "Sorry, honey. Daddy will be here soon to get you guys, so I need you to do your homework now."

Amanda pouted. "But Mom ..."

Cassie frowned and fixed stern eyes on her daughter. "Now."

Amanda sighed loudly. Even at the age of ten, she was well on her way to being a moody teenager. "Bye, Cammie. See you on Monday."

Cammie shrugged. "Have fun at your dad's house."

Cassie waited until her daughter had walked up the stairs to the front porch and into the house before closing the door behind both of them. She heard the telltale thump of Amanda's backpack being dropped onto one of the kitchen chairs and her binder slapping down on the kitchen table. As unhappy as Amanda sounded, at least Cassie didn't have to hound her about her homework like she had to with Jace.

"Jace?" Cassie said to her son's back. He didn't answer, so she moved closer. "Jace!"

He kept building, and she waved her hand in front of his face. "Hey, buddy, it's time to do your homework."

He turned slightly toward her, but didn't look up to meet her eyes. "Can I do it later?"

She sighed. "Nope."

He groaned loudly. Cassie fought to keep her patience as he precisely lined up the Lego car he'd been building with the edges of another Lego project, then sorted a small pile of loose bricks by color and moved them to the back of the table to be used later.

Finally, she got him settled onto the couch in the living room and retrieved his math homework out of his bag. "Okay, looks like you need to finish this page." She handed him the page of math problems and a clipboard to write on. Having him do his homework on the couch wasn't ideal, but she'd learned long ago not to have him work near his sister. They tended to get into fights that resulted in neither of them getting anything done.

"Fine." He picked up the pencil and leaned back on the couch. If she left him alone, maybe he'd start working. She went into the bathroom to give it a quick shine before her guests arrived. After spraying the mirror with Windex and wiping it with a cloth, she paused to listen for the scratch of Jace's pencil. Nothing.

The homework battles with Jace were one of her least favorite parts of being a mother, but it wasn't something she could avoid. He was a smart kid and could easily finish his math in five minutes, but he routinely stretched the task to over an hour. What would it be like if he was normal like Amanda?

She pressed her lips together, and her chest tightened with guilt, an all-too-familiar feeling. Jace was Jace, and she loved him no matter what —but, sometimes, being his mother was exhausting.

At least tonight she had the Wedding Crashers meeting to look forward to. Back when she was still married and decorating cakes on the side, she'd met a group of other women in the wedding industry. They decided to form a club, jokingly referring to themselves as the Wedding Crashers because they attended so many strangers' weddings. Having her friends over always brightened her spirits.

She poked her head into the living room. Jace appeared to be working, so she went back into the kitchen and took bowls out of the cupboards for chips and dip, then reached into the fridge for the sour cream. She hummed to herself as she got lost in the task of preparing snacks.

"Mom!" Amanda shouted from the table. "I'm trying to do my homework."

"Sorry, sweetie." Cassie glanced at her daughter. "Are you almost done? Daddy will be here soon."

Amanda sighed and set down her pencil. "I'm done now. Can I go to my room and read until it's time to go?"

Cassie nodded. Amanda threw her books and homework back in her backpack and ran upstairs with it. It was probably time to check on Jace's progress too. Cassie went back into the living room and sat down next to him on the couch. Her stomach knotted as she saw his math was only halfway done.

"Honey, you've got to finish this." She should have stayed with him to help, but she was always hoping that as he got older, he'd learn to complete things on his own.

"I've been working on it." He stared at the paper.

She took a deep breath. "Okay. Let's figure this out together." With her keeping him on track, he was done in ten minutes. "Awesome job, Jace. Your teacher is going to be so proud of you."

"Okay." He stood. "Can I work on my Legos now?"

"For a couple of minutes, until Daddy gets here."

He ran over to the Legos without saying anything to

her. She gathered up his schoolwork and stuck it in his backpack for him, then returned to the kitchen. The cake she'd made for tonight sat against the back counter, ready to be eaten after they polished off the appetizers everyone brought. She was trying out a new dark chocolate recipe to serve at the Willa Bay Lodge, and the Wedding Crashers would be the guinea pigs.

Her friends were due at six thirty. Kyle was supposed to pick the kids up at six, but by the time her first guest showed up, he still wasn't there.

"Kyle isn't here yet to get the kids," she said in greeting to Meg who was first to arrive.

Meg's lips formed an *O* as she looked past Cassie into the house. "What time was he supposed to get them?"

"About half an hour ago." Cassie frowned. This was typical of Kyle. He never seemed to value her time or her plans. It was one of the biggest reasons they'd divorced.

"Well, I'm sure he'll be here soon." Meg walked into the living room carrying a foil-wrapped tray and a bottle of Merlot. "Hey, Jace."

He didn't appear to hear Meg's greeting. Meg shrugged and followed Cassie into the kitchen, setting the tray on the counter and the bottle of wine next to a Chardonnay that Cassie had taken out of the fridge.

Cassie eyed the foil-wrapped container. Meg was an amazing chef, and you never knew what she was going to come up with. "What did you bring tonight?"

Meg slid the foil off the tray. "Bacon wrapped dates and a spinach artichoke quiche. I tried it out last week for a catered brunch, and Taylor just about swooned over it."

Cassie grinned. "I'll *bet* he did." She'd long felt that the head chef at the Lodge's restaurant had feelings for Meg that weren't strictly professional.

Meg's mouth dropped open. "He's my boss."

"I know, but that doesn't mean he doesn't have a thing for you." Cassie pulled a stack of plates down from an upper cabinet. "I've seen the way he looks at you."

"You're such a romantic. There's nothing like that between us." Meg sighed and pointed at the oven. "Do you mind if I pop the quiche in there to heat it up?"

"Be my guest. It's a little finicky with the temperature, though, so you'll need to watch it carefully so it doesn't burn."

Meg turned the knob to 350 degrees and set the tin on the middle rack. "Noted." She turned back to Cassie. "How do you bake cakes at home then?"

Cassie laughed. "I don't. George has always let me bake the cakes in the Lodge's kitchen."

Meg tilted her head to one side. "How come I've never seen them there?"

"Because I get to work at the crack of dawn, and you usually mosey in around noon." Cassie grinned at her. She wasn't fond of the early morning hours she worked, but the Lodge needed fresh-baked goods for breakfast and it allowed her to be home when the kids got out of school. A part-time nanny came to her house early in the morning to stay with the kids until it was time for them to wake up, then helped them get ready for school.

"I don't see you there until ten every night either." Meg narrowed her eyes at Cassie, then laughed.

"Touché."

The doorbell rang, and they looked at each other.

"Maybe that's Kyle?" Meg asked.

"It'd better be," Cassie grumbled. She hurried through the living room and flung open the door. Kyle stood on the front porch with a placid expression on his face, his hands resting in the pockets of his green windbreaker.

"Are the kids ready?" he asked.

"You're late." She knew she should be the bigger person and brush off his tardiness, but it had been a stressful day, and she didn't feel like it.

"Sorry." He gave her the lopsided grin that used to make her insides melt, but now just infuriated her. "I was finishing up a tax return. We're absolutely swamped right now."

She closed her eyes briefly. He used his long hours at a local CPA firm as an excuse all too often. She shoved her frustrations down. This wasn't the time to get into it with him. "Okay, but next time, can you please call to let me know you're going to be late? I'm hosting the Wedding Crashers tonight."

"Oh, just the girls? I'm sure they don't mind." He stepped past her into the house, leaving her to bristle at the way he'd brushed off her concerns.

"I'll go get Amanda. She's in her room, reading." Cassie stalked away from him and went upstairs to knock on Amanda's door.

"Come in," Amanda called out.

Cassie pushed the door open and Amanda looked up. "Is it time to go?" she asked.

"Yep. Are you all packed up?" Cassie jutted her chin at the small purple suitcase next to Amanda's bed. The kids stayed with her ex-husband every other weekend in the two-bedroom apartment in town that he'd rented after the divorce. He had most of what they'd need, but there were always a few things that couldn't be duplicated.

"Uh-huh." Amanda marked her page with a bookmark and stuck the book in her backpack. "Are we having dinner at Dad's tonight?"

"I certainly hope so." Cassie's teeth ached from

clenching her jaw. "Your dad told me earlier he was going to get pizza."

"Oh, yay! I love going to Dad's place." Amanda slung her backpack over her shoulders and bounced out of her bedroom. Cassie sighed under her breath and followed her daughter down the stairs, carrying the purple suitcase. The kids always liked going to Kyle's apartment because he got to be the fun dad on the weekend while she had to be the rule enforcer during the week. It didn't seem fair.

Kyle and Jace stood by the door, waiting for Amanda. Cassie hugged and kissed each of her children.

"Bye, kids. See you on Sunday."

"Bye, Mom," Amanda called over her shoulder as she skipped down the walkway to Kyle's car. Jace walked away without a word.

"See you on Sunday." Kyle flashed her that infuriating grin again and strode out to his car, twirling his keys between his fingers. Cassie took a few deep breaths and waved at the kids, who were now in the car.

Meg's mom, Debbie, and Meg's sisters, Samantha and Libby, pulled up to the curb as Kyle's car disappeared around the corner at the end of the street. They approached Cassie's house carrying plates and bowls full of appetizers. The three women ran a catering company together, although Sam also worked as a PE teacher at the local high school. Having friends with advanced cooking skills was a definite plus to working in the hospitality industry. Cassie stepped out onto the porch to help them, her mouth watering in anticipation of whatever they'd whipped up for tonight's party.

"Hey, Cass." Debbie gave Cassie a one-armed hug while carefully balancing the green Tupperware bowl she held. "How's it going? Was that Kyle's car we saw pulling out of here?"

"Yep." Cassie tried to relax her breathing. She wasn't going to let her ex-husband ruin her evening. "The kids went to his place for the weekend."

Libby hugged her too, her dark hair swinging around her shoulders in smooth waves like something right out of a shampoo commercial. Cassie had always been envious of Meg's older sister when they were growing up, and if Libby wasn't so nice, it would be easy to hate her. "That must be tough for you. Right now, it sounds like heaven to have my kids gone for the weekend, but I know I'd miss them like crazy."

"The first few times without them were hard," Cassie said. "But I'm starting to enjoy having time for myself on Kyle's weekends. Last week, I even went to an art museum in Seattle. I haven't done that since college."

Debbie nodded. "I remember when my girls left home for college. I thought being an empty nester was the end of the world, but I started to see its advantages." She eyed her youngest daughter, Samantha, and laughed. "Although I guess I didn't have much to worry about. I can't seem to get rid of any of them now."

Libby mock-glared at her mother, but Cassie saw her pat Debbie's arm with affection.

"Is everyone else here?" Samantha asked.

"Meg's here, but Celia and Zoe are running a little late. I think Zoe had some work thing to do." Cassie took one of the casserole dishes from Samantha as they all walked inside the house.

Meg was waiting just inside the door and gave her mom a big hug as she entered.

"What was that for?" Debbie tilted her head up to look at Meg, who was several inches taller than her.

Meg shrugged. "I'm just glad to be home with all of you right now."

Libby walked past them while they were hugging and murmured under her breath, "It took you long enough to come home."

Her words were so soft that Cassie wondered if she'd heard her correctly. It wasn't like Libby to be negative, though, so Cassie pushed the thought out of her mind as they all moved through the living room to the kitchen.

"Well, we're glad you're here too." Debbie set the green bowl on the counter and removed the lid. "I brought my famous chicken salad."

"The one with the grapes in it?" Cassie perked up. "I love that salad."

"Yes." Debbie sat down on one of the high-backed chairs at the kitchen table.

The front door squeaked, but before Cassie could get past her friends to see who had arrived, Zoe's voice sang out from the living room as she walked toward them. "Hey, everyone. Celia and I let ourselves in. Sorry we're a little late." She walked into the kitchen and set a crudités platter on the table. Celia, Zoe's landlord, paused in the kitchen doorway, her gnarled hand curved around the handle of a wooden cane.

"You're not late at all," Cassie said as she pulled one of the kitchen chairs out from the table. "Celia, why don't you have a seat over here?"

"Thank you." Celia slowly lowered herself into the chair.. Up until a few years ago, she hadn't seemed to age. Once she'd hit eighty and her eyes had started to fail, she'd slowed noticeably. She'd stopped driving then, so every Sunday, Cassie picked her up to take her to the Lutheran church they both attended. Kyle had the kids every other weekend, so it was nice having company on the way to and from church.

"Thanks for hosting this, Cassie." Celia picked up a carrot stick from the platter in front of her and dipped it in some ranch dressing. "I always look forward to these evenings."

"Me too." Zoe pulled up a chair next to her. "I spend all day talking to people, but it's nice to be around friends."

"How are things going at the Lodge?" Libby asked. "Joan's retiring soon, right? Did George say anything about a promotion?"

"No." Zoe's brow furrowed. "Not yet."

"I'm sure he'll talk to you about it soon," Meg said.

Cassie moved the rest of the appetizers over to the kitchen table and brought a chair in from the living room for herself.

"Oh!" Debbie gasped. "Speaking of George, did you hear that Lara Camden is moving back to Willa Bay? Her mom, Greta, told me yesterday. Greta and George are over the moon about it. I think they're hoping for some grandchildren in the next few years." She looked pointedly at Meg and Samantha. "I know what that's like."

"Oh, Mom." Meg shook her head.

"Yeah, you're going to be waiting for a while if you're expecting grandchildren from Meg or me. Brant and I aren't planning on having kids for at least a few years after we're married." Samantha gave Libby a sly grin, then laughed. "Besides, Libby's given you four already. Isn't that enough?"

Debbie shook her head. "Nope. I can't wait until I have enough grandchildren to play flag football at Thanksgiving. I used to love doing that when I was a kid."

Her expression darkened for a moment. "I hope I'm around to see that."

"You will be, Mom." Meg patted her arm. "I'm sure of it."

"Well, we'll know next week when I get the results back from the scan." Debbie clasped her hands together and smiled at them. "Enough of that kind of talk though."

Cassie searched for something to say to change the subject. "So, Lara's really coming back to town?"

"According to her mom." Debbie leaned in closer to the group. "I heard her husband got fired from his last job, and they had to move home with her parents for a while."

Samantha snorted. "And he's planning on finding a job in Willa Bay? Good luck with that. Brant's been looking for something closer ever since he moved here."

"I don't know about you, but I'd be happier if Lara Camden had stayed away for good." Meg scooped up some chicken salad with a celery stick and bit into it with a loud crunch. "She's always trying to stir up trouble," she said around the bite. After she swallowed it, she turned to Cassie. "Remember that time she cheated off of you in math and then blamed you?"

Cassie's stomach soured. Lara had copied her answers on a math test, and when she'd been caught, she'd told the teacher that Cassie was in on it. They'd both been given two weeks of detention, and Cassie's parents had been furious, grounding her for months.

Libby rolled her eyes. "Yeah, or when she took advantage of Cassie being grounded and tried to make Kyle take her to the prom?"

Long-forgotten anger boiled up as Cassie thought about Lara's attempt to steal her boyfriend. Kyle had told Lara off and won Cassie's heart in the process. She'd decided right then and there that he was the man she was going to marry. It was funny to think that Lara's actions had cemented Cassie and Kyle's relationship. If Lara hadn't cheated on that test, would Cassie's life be different now?

"Wow, I've never met Lara before, but I'll try to steer clear." Zoe shivered. "She sounds like a real piece of work."

"No kidding," Samantha said. "I've heard stories about her, but I was still in elementary school when all of that went down. I remember how mad Meg was about it though."

Cassie took a calming breath and mentally counted to ten. On top of the divorce, single parenthood, and having little time to spare, she had been warned by her doctor that her blood pressure was creeping up too high. She pasted a smile on her face. "I'm sure she's changed. Maybe she'll be completely different than she used to be."

"I hope so." Debbie's gaze was heavy on Cassie's face, and Cassie braced herself for bad news. "I wasn't sure how to tell you this, but it's better you find out sooner rather than later. Her mom said Lara plans to open up a bakery in town and make wedding cakes."

Ice shot through Cassie's veins, and she struggled to get control of her thoughts. Demand was strong for wedding cakes in Willa Bay, but she was barely making ends meet as it was. If she lost any clients to Lara's new business, she may not be able to make her mortgage.

Zoe sensed her dismay. "You have nothing to worry about, Cassie. Everyone knows you make the best cakes in town." She stood from the table and walked over to the bottles Meg had lined up on the counter. "Can I interest anyone in a glass of wine?"

Everyone's hands shot up except Debbie's. "Not me. I

have to drive, and after not drinking for so long, I'm such a lightweight."

Libby lowered her hand. "Mom, I can drive you home if you want a glass of wine. After spending the day at the hospital, you deserve it."

Debbie eyed her oldest daughter first, then the wine bottle Zoe was tilting back and forth suggestively. Her lips spread into a wide smile. "Oh, all right. I guess I do deserve something. Give me a small glass of the red." Zoe started pouring, and Debbie laughed. "Oh heck. I'm not driving. Fill it up to the top." She grabbed the full glass from Zoe and took a long swig of wine. "I really hate those scans."

"I'll take the red wine too," Celia said. "You know, studies have shown it's good for you to have a glass a day. We all want to stay healthy, right?"

Everyone chuckled, and Zoe handed Celia a glass of merlot. The rest of them got their drinks and settled in at the table. Cassie sat back in her chair, enjoying the sounds of laughter as everyone relaxed and got into a festive mood.

"How's the Gustafson wedding going, Zoe?" Debbie asked. "Diana is one of the most demanding brides I've ever met. I think we've changed the catering menu at least twenty times."

Zoe sighed. "Not well. I thought we had a plan for the ceremony, but like the catering, she's changed it so many times already. I don't know if it's her mom's influence or she's just indecisive, but I'm getting tired of it."

"Maybe I should be glad I didn't get the contract for the wedding cake." Cassie gulped her wine, hoping it would take away some of her stress. "She and her mother tried every type of cake I make, but decided to go with someone else."

"Sounds like you dodged a bullet there." Meg reached for a chip and dipped it in the salsa. "And now that we're on the topic of cakes, when do we get to dig into that beauty on the counter? Or did you set it there just to torture us?" Her eyes danced as she cast a teasing glare at Cassie.

Cassie stood, her pulse quickening. Serving an untested recipe was always nerve-wracking, even when it was only to her friends. "Nope, it's for tonight. It's something new I'm trying out." She picked up the chocolate cake. "Does anyone want some?"

Everyone raised their hands and she brought the cake over to the table before slicing it and giving them each a piece.

"This is amazing." Zoe swallowed her last bite and reached for the cake server to get more.

Cassie's chest filled with pride. "Thank you. I'm glad you like it." She cut into her own piece of cake with a fork, scrutinizing the texture. It was moist with a good crumb, always a good sign. She took a small bite and let the decadent chocolate ganache filling melt onto her tongue. Yep. This one was a keeper.

Meg set her fork down and rubbed her flat stomach. "Oh man, that was delicious, but I'm stuffed now. You're going to have to roll me into work tomorrow."

"Me too." Debbie yawned. "I think I need to get home soon. I'm wiped out after being at the hospital today."

Libby jumped up. "I'd better get home myself and make sure Gabe has the kids in bed. It's getting late."

"Well, you're my ride, so I guess I'm leaving too." Samantha stuffed a last bite of cake into her mouth, then pouted at her empty plate. "Cassie, can I get this recipe from you sometime? Brant loves chocolate."

"Sure." Cassie beamed. "I'll email it to you tonight. I

found the basic recipe online, but I made a few tweaks to it."

Samantha and her mom left with Libby, and Meg walked out with them, carrying her mom's serving bowl.

"Do you need any help?" Zoe asked Cassie.

Cassie looked around the kitchen. They hadn't made too big of a mess, and since the kids weren't going to be home until Sunday, she had plenty of time to clean up. "No, I'm good."

Zoe eyed the kitchen with doubt. "If you're sure."

"I am." Cassie grinned at her. "This was fun though. I wish we could get together more than once a month."

"Me too." Celia pushed herself up from the table and leaned on her cane. "Being around all of you young people makes me feel young again too – at least for a few hours." She sighed. "But it does make me a little nostalgic hearing about everything that's going on in town. I miss being in the thick of wedding season."

"I have more than enough work if you'd like some." Zoe winked at Celia. "In fact, maybe you could come in with me one day and distract Diana Gustafson's mother so I can root out what Diana actually wants for her wedding."

A smile formed on Celia's thin lips, smoothing out the wrinkles in her rouged cheeks. "I'd like that."

They all walked outside together. Cassie stood on the porch and waved goodbye as Zoe helped Celia into the passenger seat of her car. When they were out of sight, Cassie went back inside and into the kitchen.

She hadn't been lying – there wasn't that much of a mess. When all of the food was packed away in the refrigerator and cupboard, she wiped away a few crumbs and sat down with a second piece of cake and a cup of decaf coffee. She bit into the cake, and although she'd liked it earlier, now it tasted too sweet. She pushed the plate away. The news of Lara Camden's impending return to Willa Bay had been unsettling. What if she lost clients to Lara? Without that income, she wasn't sure how she'd make ends meet. After the divorce, she'd worked hard to make a life for herself in Willa Bay, but now she feared that all she'd built could soon come crashing down around her.

3
_____

Zoe

When Celia was settled into the passenger seat, Zoe slowly pulled away from the curb outside of Cassie's house. When they'd arrived at the gathering, it had still been light outside, but now the sky was dark and drizzling. She turned on the windshield wipers to clear the raindrops accumulating on the glass. Next to her, Celia rubbed her leg and moaned softly.

A ribbon of fear shot through Zoe. She stopped the car in the middle of the empty street and eyed the elderly woman. "Are you okay?"

Celia pressed her lips together for a moment, then nodded. "I'm fine. It's just my arthritis acting up again."

"Is it the change in the weather?" Zoe asked. "My grandfather always says his knee aches more when it starts to rain." She eased her foot off of the brake, moving forward slowly as she continued to surreptitiously check on Celia.

Celia shook her head. "I'm not sure what it is. I've been having to use my cane more and more because my leg feels a little weak at times."

Zoe returned her full attention to the road. Celia was fiercely protective of her independence and wouldn't take too kindly to meddling, but Zoe wanted to make sure her elderly neighbor was safe. "Do you need any help at the house? I'm happy to come over to clean or do other chores if you need it."

Celia's words were full of steel. "Thank you, dear, but I can take care of my own house."

"Well if you ever need any help, just let me know. I'm right next door to you."

"Of course, dear." Celia sighed softly and her voice trembled a little. "I feel like I'm already taking advantage of you and the others too much. You shouldn't have to drive around an old lady. All of you are too busy for that."

Zoe turned down the gravel driveway leading to her cottage and the old Willa Bay Inn. "It's not any trouble. I don't mind driving you places, and I know the others are happy to help in any way they can. You've been so kind to all of us over the years."

Celia didn't answer but stared out the window while they lurched around the holes in the driveway. Although she'd lived on Celia's property for years, Zoe realized she didn't know much about her. Celia tended to be closemouthed about her own past.

The few times Zoe had been a guest in Celia's home, their conversations had centered around what Willa Bay had been like back in the day. As air travel became more common, fewer people came to stay at the local resorts, which foundered until they rebranded themselves as highly regarded destinations for weddings. According to people who'd grown up in Willa Bay, Celia had been instrumental in that transformation.

"Have you ever thought about selling this property?" Zoe asked.

Celia yanked her gaze away from the trees and stared at Zoe as if she'd grown a horn on top of her head. "I'm going to live on this property until the day I die. This is the only true home I've ever known."

Zoe cringed at the sharpness in Celia's tone. She hadn't meant to offend the older woman and hoped it wouldn't affect their relationship in the future. She parked the car in front of the blue Victorian mansion, turned the engine off, and stepped out into a mud puddle. She cursed under her breath and came around to Celia's side to open the car door for her.

Celia carefully lifted her legs out and set her feet on the ground, then firmly planted her cane and pushed herself up to standing. "You don't need to fuss over me."

Zoe just smiled and closed the car door, walking a few steps behind Celia as she made her way up the steps to the front door. Celia fiddled with her keys, her fingers refusing to pick out the correct one. Zoe hung back, resisting the urge to help her. Finally, Celia had the key in hand and inserted it into the lock, pushing on the antique brass doorknob until the door swung open with a loud creak.

Celia leaned against the doorframe. "Thanks for the ride, Zoe. I had a good time with all of you girls." She took a long breath like she was going to say something else, but pressed her lips together instead.

"Goodnight," Zoe said.

"Goodnight." Celia closed the door behind her.

Zoe drove the short distance down the road to her cottage and let herself inside. The air in the small living room had a chill to it because she'd turned off the heat at the beginning of April. The temperatures were still in the low fifties at night, but she refused to turn the furnace back on again until next winter, even if it wouldn't have taken much to warm up the small cottage.

It had been a long time since Zoe had lived with a roommate, and she didn't really want one, but there were still evenings like tonight where she was keenly aware of the remote and quiet atmosphere of the cottage.

She curled up on the couch, clutching a turquoise throw pillow to her chest, and flipped on the TV. After the earlier high of being with her friends, she needed some background noise to make her feel a little less alone. Sometimes she wondered if she'd ever have someone to share her life with, but for now, she was content with her job at the Lodge and her little cottage by the sea.

~

Celia

Celia waved goodbye to Zoe, then closed the front door, obscuring the light from the car's headlights. She leaned on her cane to keep Pebbles, her overly enthusiastic gray-and-white terrier, from knocking her off-balance. Running her fingers over the familiar ridges on the wallpaper next to the door, she found the light switch and flipped it on.

Pebbles bounced on the rug by her feet, and she bent down to pet him. The little dog always brought a smile to her face. He'd been a stray that had shown up on her friend Elizabeth's porch one day, and Celia had fallen in love with him the first time she laid eyes on him.

"C'mon, Pebbles. Let's get you some dinner." Sometimes she felt odd talking to a dog, but her husband, Charlie, had been gone for ten years. It had to be better than having long conversations with herself.

Pebbles trotted along beside her. The pattering of his little feet and the thumping of her cane beat out a rhythm on the scarred hardwood flooring as they made their way to the kitchen. Framed pictures lined the hallway – formal portraits of Charlie and her, favorite guests that had stayed at the inn, and one of her prized possessions: a photo of herself with the Wedding Crashers group after a successful fundraiser for the local food bank. She'd known Elizabeth Arnold, Elizabeth's daughter Debbie, and Debbie's girls for years. But it was through her volunteer work with the chamber of commerce that she'd met Zoe, Cassie, and the rest of the younger members of the local hospitality-industry community.

Although she and Charlie had always wanted children, they'd never been blessed with them. She'd often wondered if her actions in the past were to blame for their inability to have children, but when she'd confessed her worries to Charlie, he'd held her in his arms and told her that was ridiculous. Oh, how she missed that sweet man.

A movement at the end of the hallway caught her attention, and Celia looked straight into the antique mirror that had been there for as long as she could remember. Although she'd slowed down in recent years, she'd always felt young at heart. However, the mirror revealed an elderly woman with curly white hair stooping over a cane. She touched the tips of her fingers to her face, and her reflection did the same. Her skin was soft from the cold cream she applied nightly but etched with wrinkles. Not for the first time she wondered, *when did I get so old?*

Pebbles nudged her leg, and she shook her head. It didn't matter how she looked. She was still living independently in her own house and didn't plan to leave anytime soon – even if Zoe and her other young friends evidently thought she needed help. This had been her home for over sixty years, even before she'd married Charlie and they'd taken over the operation of the Inn at Willa Bay together.

Memories of the Inn at its peak filled her thoughts as she dumped a scoop of dog food into Pebbles's bowl. He was chomping away even before the last piece of kibble landed.

She poured cold, day-old coffee into her favorite mug, grinning at the Maxine comic imprinted on the front of it. The old biddy reminded her that getting old had its perks – you didn't have to worry anymore about what other people thought of you.

Celia shuffled back to the living room with her coffee and sat down heavily in her favorite recliner, then aimed the remote at the television. Pebbles finished eating, and raced into the room, leaping onto her lap before the aging television had even flickered on. Since he'd come into her life, they'd settled into their own nightly routine. Per their usual arrangement, she scooted to the side to give him more room, and they settled down to watch whatever sitcom happened to be on.

She sipped her coffee slowly. Her life may not be as exciting as when she'd managed the most popular resort in all of Willa Bay, but she was happy with it. She had friends, a canine companion, food in her belly, and a roof over her head. What more could anyone ask for?

A commercial came on, and her eyes drifted to the

stack of bills sitting on her desk causing the coffee in her stomach to turn to acid. She quickly averted her eyes and reached out to pet Pebbles. Things had always worked out in the past, and there was no reason they wouldn't this time.

4

Meg

"Taylor." Meg waited in the doorway of the Willa Bay Lodge's executive chef's office, just off the kitchen. Taylor Argo's head continued to bop, most likely keeping time with the beat of his beloved country music. The headphones he wore over his ears to block out background noise while doing administrative tasks worked all too well.

Meg grinned. It always cracked her up when she caught him dancing or singing along to his music. Working for Taylor was one of the few things she loved about her job at the Lodge. He'd recently been named as one of the top ten chefs under forty in the Northwest, but unlike most of the executive chefs she'd worked for in Portland, he was casual and down-to-earth. On her first day as a sous-chef at the Lodge, she'd addressed him as Chef. He'd laughed and told her that it wasn't a big enough restaurant for such formality, and she should call him by his first name.

She walked in and tapped him on the shoulder.

He jumped in his chair, then ripped off his headphones. The movement made his gelled black hair spike out even more wildly than normal. "Dude. You scared me." He rolled his chair back a little and looked up at her. "What's up?"

"The vegetable delivery came, but they were out of eggplants." She glanced at the screen, curious to see if he was working on a new menu. One never knew what he was going to come up with, which made even the locals come back week after week to try out his newest creation.

He reached for the printed menu he'd set on the corner of his desk, his long, slender fingers dwarfing the paper as he scanned the contents. "Well that's going to make it difficult to make the gluten-free lasagna tonight."

"I know. I was thinking we could use zucchini instead. Cassie has a bunch that she was going to make bread out of for breakfast, but I'm sure she can do something else if we need it."

He eyed her thoughtfully and tapped the arm of his chair. "Good thinking. Let's do it."

She beamed. "I'll let Cassie know, and I'll get started prepping the lasagnas." The Lodge may not have been Michelin-rated, but it felt good for a talented chef like Taylor to recognize her for her menu ideas.

Meg rinsed off the zucchinis in a large colander and set it on the prep counter. One by one, she trimmed and cut them into precise, thin slices with a mandoline. The work was monotonous, but there was something calming about preparing vegetables, and she enjoyed seeing the growing piles of perfectly cut zucchini.

When she'd finished, she salted the zucchini to draw out the moisture and laid the faux noodles out on a cloth while she got to work on the Bolognese sauce for the lasagna. Her mind wandered as she stirred Italian seasonings into the mounds of beef, celery, carrots, onions, and garlic that were already in the pan, the herbs adding another layer to the tantalizing aroma into the air.

She'd always loved cooking, ever since the first time her Nana Elizabeth had taught her how to make pancakes. Nana had referred to the first pancake as the "try" pancake – a way to test if the griddle was hot enough, the batter was the right consistency, or if they'd added enough vanilla and cinnamon. Cooking with her grandmother had taught her that not everything would turn out correctly the first time, but almost any mistake in the kitchen could be fixed.

With the beef mixture browned, she added tomatoes and put a lid on it to simmer. She returned to the zucchini, squeezing it in cheesecloth to remove any excess moisture, and began laying it in the bottom of a large baking tray. The dinner rush wouldn't start for a few hours, but lasagna took a while to prepare, so they always did it well ahead of time. She checked the Bolognese sauce and lowered the temperature slightly.

With that done, she began washing vegetables for the dinner salads. She was just about to rinse a head of romaine lettuce when her phone rang in the pocket of her double-breasted white chef's jacket. Normally, she wouldn't answer it while she was in the middle of a kitchen task, but, although it would be unlikely on a Sunday, she worried that it could be her mother calling to relay news from her doctor.

She didn't recognize the number. "Hello?"

"Hello," a chipper voice rang out. "I'm calling to notify you that you've won a free vacation to Hawaii."

Meg sighed and hung up the phone. Telemarketers. There was a reason she didn't answer the phone at work.

Being distracted while holding a sharp knife wasn't a smart idea.

She grabbed the lettuce and colander and returned to rinsing away any dirt, but the phone call had disturbed her peace of mind. When was her mom going to hear from the doctor anyway? He'd told Debbie that he'd contact her sometime this week, but that could mean anywhere from Monday through Friday. It was going to be a long week for everyone in the Briggs family.

Meg closed her eyes for a moment. The scans would come back clear, and her mom was going to be fine.

When her mom had called to tell her that she'd been diagnosed with breast cancer, Meg had been working as a sous-chef at a prestigious restaurant in Portland. Although her career trajectory had been promising there, worrying about her mother had been too distracting, and Meg knew she'd regret not moving home if something happened. Family was more important than anything else.

She'd been lucky to find the job at the Willa Bay Lodge, but it was a small restaurant, and as far as she knew, Taylor had no intention of leaving anytime soon. There were many good restaurants in Willa Bay, but the story was pretty much the same everywhere else – in a small town, people stayed in their jobs until they were ready to retire.

"Hey, Meg," Cassie said.

Startled, Meg looked up. "You're not working today, right?"

Cassie smiled. "Not here. But I've got a cake in the fridge for a client's wedding tonight, and I need to deliver it."

"Need any help?" Meg scanned the counter and stove. Everything was on track for dinner. "I can take a break."

"That would be great." Some of the tension left Cassie's shoulders. "The bride wanted a six-tier cake, and it came out bigger than I'd expected. I was wondering how I'd manage it myself."

They entered the walk-in refrigerator together, and Meg helped Cassie lift the piece of plywood that she'd built the cake on. They took slow steps in unison as they neared the kitchen door. Cassie pushed her back against the door to open it. As they walked down the back hallway and out the door, Meg half-expected one of the office doors to open suddenly and cause the cake to catapult to the floor.

Luckily, they made it to Cassie's van without incident. Cassie had removed the back seats to allow room for the cake, and once it was safely ensconced in the vehicle, she shut the back liftgate.

"Do you have time to grab a cup of coffee?" Cassie asked. "I don't have to be at the wedding for another couple of hours."

Meg did a mental check on the status of everything in the kitchen. "Yeah. I could do with a latte. Let me tell Taylor I'm heading out for my lunch break, so he can keep an eye on the Bolognese sauce." She started walking back to the Lodge and Cassie followed her.

"Ooh. I love your Bolognese sauce." Cassie's stomach grumbled audibly. "Are you serving it with the linguini noodles like you did last week?"

"Nope. We're testing out a new menu tonight. Zucchini lasagna." Meg smiled with pride. "Oh, by the way, I'm using up all the zucchini if that's okay with you."

"That's fine. It sounds really good. Maybe not as delicious as real noodles, but I'm sure it'll be great." Cassie paused when they got to the kitchen. "I'll wait here while you check in with Taylor. Have you seen Zoe today?"

Meg nodded. "She's out in the garden." She looked up at the big round clock on the wall. "There's a wedding starting in about twenty minutes."

"Ah. I'm going to sneak a peek of the wedding if you don't mind." Cassie blushed. "I just love weddings. They're so full of romance and hope for the future."

Meg laughed. "And then it all comes crashing down." She'd never understood the allure of a big wedding ceremony and reception. When it came time for her own wedding, which might never happen at the rate she was going, she wanted only a small ceremony with close friends and family.

Cassie grimaced. "True. I thought what Kyle and I had would last forever. Little did I know forever only meant ten years." She sighed. "I hope I find love like that again – the good parts, I mean, not the bad."

Meg gave her a quick hug. "I know you will. Any man would be lucky to have you in his life."

A cloud of sadness came over Cassie's face. "Maybe someday. Right now, I have too much on my plate to even think about finding someone new." She closed her eyes for a moment, then opened them and smiled weakly at Meg. "I'll meet you outside, okay?"

"I'll be there in a minute." Meg walked over to Taylor's office door and rapped on it sharply.

"Come in," Taylor called out. He'd removed his headphones, but he was staring at the computer screen. "I'm still trying to figure out next week's menu. The cost of beef went up so much last week that I'm thinking we may need to cut back a little. I hate to pass the cost on to our customers."

She crossed the room to look over his shoulder. He moved aside slightly to allow her a better view of the computer monitor, and she caught a pleasant whiff of his aftershave.

She pointed to one of the entrées. "What if we replace the filet mignon with salmon? I know that halibut is in season, and we wanted to offer it as our seafood dish, but we could do a nice salmon with a lemon-caper cream sauce too. We'll still have the beef stroganoff for people who want beef, but it will give us something at a lower price point." It was a fine line to walk between the higher-priced menu items that the tourists were willing to pay for and what the locals could afford. One of the owner's core beliefs was that the Lodge should have an accessible special-occasion restaurant for locals, not just out-of-town guests.

A wide smile crossed Taylor's face. "I love it. Thanks, Meg. You're really saving the day today." He clicked the cell with filet mignon in it, replacing it with the salmon dish.

She stepped back from the desk, pride welling up in her chest. Creating the menu was something she looked forward to doing when she eventually moved up to a head chef position. Back in Portland, she never would have been encouraged to have any input on the menu, but Taylor seemed to value her opinion, even if he did have the final say.

"I'm going to head out for lunch with Cassie, if that's okay with you." With him sitting in the office chair, she had to tilt her head down to meet his eyes – a weird feeling because he was over six feet in height, and even being tall herself, she was used to looking up at him. She'd never taken notice of the warmth in his dark-brown eyes before, or how the corners of his mouth crinkled pleasantly when he smiled.

She shook her head. Cassie's comment about Taylor

having a crush on her was starting to get to her. He was her boss, and she was only interested in him professionally.

"Yep, it's fine with me." He gestured to his screen. "I'm almost finished here."

She backed up until she was standing in the open doorway, eager to put some distance between them and the confusing thoughts about him that had just popped into her head. "The sauce for the lasagna is simmering on the stove. Can you check on it while I'm gone? I should be back in thirty minutes."

"Will do." He looked like he was about to say something else, but went back to the menu planning.

Meg gave the sauce one last stir and went out the service exit to the gardens. A small wedding – probably under fifty people – had been set up in the Pergola Garden. Rows of white chairs were bisected by a wide aisle leading up to the picturesque archway overlooking the water. Violet ribbons lined the chairs along the aisle, and white roses intertwined with purple flowers she didn't recognize adorned the cross-hatching of the pergola. It was beautiful in its simplicity, something Zoe had a gift for creating.

Zoe was in full event coordinator mode, stalking from one end of the gardens to the other while relaying instructions to the grounds crew and the catering staff. A woman in a pink lace dress, who Meg guessed to be the mother-of-the-bride, was firing questions at Zoe so fast that Meg wondered how her friend could keep up. Zoe kept her cool, though, and everything hummed along like a fine-tuned machine.

Meg caught sight of Cassie, who was hanging out in the part of the garden closest to the Lodge. She waved at Meg, who walked over to join her.

"I don't envy Zoe," Meg whispered to Cassie. "I don't know how she does it."

"Me neither," Cassie confessed. "I have some contact with the bride and groom when they're ordering the cake, but to be in charge of putting it all together?" She shivered. "That job is not for me, but Zoe will be an amazing event manager."

"Look at Zoe's face. She's so calm! If that were me, I'd be screaming at the woman she's talking with." Meg eyed the woman in the pink dress pestering Zoe, who was obviously extremely busy.

"Let's go before Zoe sees us and ropes us into helping." Cassie's eyes twinkled. She may have been kidding about Zoe asking them to help, but it had happened before. Sometimes, when everything that could go wrong did, it was all hands on deck to make sure the event got back on track. This time, though, it looked like Zoe had everything under control.

"I'm starving. Can we go to the Wedding Belles Cafe? I can get a latte and maybe a chocolate chip muffin." Meg checked her watch. "It'll only take about ten minutes to walk to town, and I could use the exercise."

"Me too." Cassie patted her stomach, which pooched out a little. "I've been testing too many new cake recipes lately. If I had time, I'd join a gym." She scrunched up her face. "Thank goodness I really don't have much extra time, or I'd have to come up with a different excuse to not exercise."

Meg laughed. She and Cassie had been friends since preschool. Cassie had always preferred to stay home baking or reading instead of riding bikes or playing outside. It had come as no surprise to anyone when Cassie had eventually gone to pastry school.

They walked the half mile to town on the sidewalk

along Willa Bay Drive. Private lanes leading to waterfront residences and B&Bs snaked off the main road, and every so often, a glimmer of blue waves showed through a gap in the trees. When they neared the point where the Willomish River emptied into the bay, the forests opened up to reveal a park with a grass field, a playground, and a paved promenade that provided public access to the river. An iron bridge painted a shade of red similar to the Golden Gate in San Francisco arched high over the water. On the other side was a marina and a boat ramp.

Meg relished the stretch in her legs as they traversed the bridge. The fitness tracker she wore told her that the exhaustion in her calves every night was warranted, but her frequent steps across the kitchen weren't the same as a long walk with variable terrain.

When they reached the main drag through town, Cassie held up her hand, breathing hard. "Give me a minute."

Meg tried hard to suppress a smile.

Cassie caught Meg's smirk and mock-glared at her. "Okay, okay. So I need to exercise more regularly."

"I didn't say anything." Meg grinned at her. "But if you want to go jogging with me sometime, I'm up for it."

Cassie stared at her feet and said in a low voice, "I may take you up on that."

Meg eyed her with surprise. She'd good-naturedly teased Cassie about her hatred of exercise for all of their lives, but she'd never heard her friend reply so seriously. "Really?"

Cassie nodded. "It's time I started taking care of myself. My stress levels are through the roof. Maybe exercise will help."

Meg put her hand on Cassie's shoulder. "Are you doing okay? For real?"

Cassie smiled, but it didn't quite meet her eyes. "I'm fine. There's just a lot going on in my life right now."

"Well, I'm here if you want to talk about it." Meg hated seeing her oldest friend like this, but she didn't know what to do for her.

"Thank you. I may take you up on that offer one of these days." Cassie gave her a more genuine grin. "For now, though, that cinnamon dolce latte is calling my name." She took off down the street, leaving Meg to jog after her.

Meg didn't want to push the issue, but she figured Cassie would talk to her about it when she was ready. Until then, Meg was glad that she'd decided to return to Willa Bay, not only to be there for her family, but to support her friends as well.

5

Zoe

"We're all set for December twenty-third." Zoe smiled at her new clients, gathering the papers they had just signed into a neat pile.

"I'm so excited!" The bride-to-be squealed and threw her arms around her fiancé's neck. "This place is absolutely perfect."

He patted her on the back with an amused smile on his face. "I'm glad you like it. I wasn't sure we'd ever find something that fulfilled all of your requirements for a venue. I was beginning to worry you didn't actually want to get married." He winked at Zoe, then kissed his fiancée to let her know he was kidding.

Zoe smothered a grin as she swiveled her chair to face the wall behind her desk and inserted the documents they'd just signed into the copier. The lovebirds were still kissing when she turned back around.

She cleared her throat. "Here you go." She held out the copies she'd made. "Feel free to call me if you have any questions, and I'll be reaching out to you in the fall to work on the details of your wedding."

"Thank you so much," the woman gushed. "I'm seriously so excited about this! My friends are going to be so jealous."

The man stood and offered his hand to his fiancée to help her up. Zoe walked them through the maze of back hallways to the main lobby. The bride-to-be never stopped smiling the entire time, and her happiness was contagious. This was a part of the job that Zoe loved – making people happy and excited about their future.

She returned to her office and recorded all the information about the couple's wedding, then reviewed the events for the upcoming week. They weren't yet in the heart of the wedding season, but things were getting busier. She had a retirement party, a fiftieth anniversary, and three weddings this week. Four out of the five events would be catered in-house, which always added another dimension to event planning.

One of the honorees at the anniversary dinner had some food allergies, and she jotted down a reminder to talk to Taylor about the menu. She'd noted the allergies previously, but she liked to double-check details like that. Having a party guest leave the Lodge in an ambulance wouldn't be good for anyone.

A flashing light on her desk phone followed by a loud ring pulled her attention away from the anniversary party to answer it. "Hello?"

"Zoe, it's George. Can you come down to my office for a minute? I want to talk to you about something."

Zoe's heart thudded so loudly that the phone receiver pressed against her ear seemed to amplify it. Was this it? Was George finally promoting her to the event manager position?

"Zoe? Are you there?"

"Yes. Sorry. I'll come down to your office right now." She hung up the phone and stood, steadying herself against the desk. Her legs wobbled, and blood pounded in her ears. She'd waited years for this opportunity, and now it was all coming true.

Zoe knocked on George's closed door.

"Come in," he said.

Zoe pushed open the door with a smile on her face, unable to hold back her excitement. She stepped inside – and stopped short.

A man was sitting across from her boss.

"Oh. I'm sorry. I didn't realize you were meeting with someone." Had she misheard George's request for her to come to his office? Maybe he'd said to come later. She glanced at the stranger, who looked vaguely familiar to her.

"Actually, I called you down here to introduce you to my son-in-law, Pearson Jones." George gestured to the man across from him. "Pearson, this is Zoe Tisdale, the Lodge's event coordinator."

This wasn't about the promotion. Her excitement deflated like an old helium balloon, but she tried to hide her disappointment. "It's nice to meet you." She held out her hand to Pearson.

He returned the handshake with limp fingers. "Nice to meet you too."

Zoe stepped back and looked at George. "I heard your daughter and son-in-law were moving back to town. That's so exciting for you all."

George gave her a tight-lipped smile. "It is. My wife is thrilled." He eyed Pearson, then looked back at Zoe and took a deep breath. "I wanted to introduce you to Pearson because he's going to be coming on board as our new event manager when Joan leaves."

Zoe froze in place, unable to do anything but stare at George. She must have heard him incorrectly. "Excuse me, but did you say he's been hired as the new event manager?"

George nodded. "Joan will begin training him tomorrow." He folded his hands on the desk, rubbing one thumb against the other but not making eye contact with her. "I've told him how great you are at your job and how lucky he'll be to have you at his side." He looked up at her. "I know the two of you will make a wonderful team."

Zoe's stomach churned from the rollercoaster of emotions. She looked over at Pearson, who flashed her an oily grin. She quickly averted her eyes. "I'm sure we will," she managed to eke out. She had to get out of there before she threw up. "I've got some things to finish up before the end of the day. Pearson, it's nice to meet you." She put her hand on the doorframe and used it to propel herself out of the office, closing the door before George could respond.

Unshed tears clouded her vision as she made her way back to her office on autopilot. She closed the door tightly behind her and collapsed into her desk chair. His son-in-law? Seriously? She'd been working toward this promotion for years and hadn't seen this coming. Now she'd be forced to work with Pearson when he took over the job that should have been hers.

She still had work to do, but when she tried to focus on the computer screen, her head throbbed, and the words swam in front of her eyes. Reluctantly, she saved the document she was working on and turned the computer off. It was after five o'clock, and while she'd usually be there for several more hours at this time of year, she decided to call it quits for the day.

Zoe grabbed her jacket from the hook by the door and peeked into the hallway to make sure it was empty. She didn't think she could handle seeing George or Pearson again that evening. If Meg or Cassie had been there, she may have ducked into the kitchen to tell them the bad news, but the restaurant was closed for dinner on Mondays, and Cassie had left hours ago.

The drive home was a blur, but Zoe's death grip on the steering wheel had her arms and hands aching by the time she pulled into the driveway leading to the old Inn and her cottage. As she passed by Celia's home, a flash of white caught her eye.

Pebbles barked and pawed frantically at her from inside the front window. Every time she'd seen the little dog before, he'd been glued to Celia's side. Icy fear arced through her heart, obliterating any thoughts of the lost promotion.

She slammed on the brakes, threw the car into park, ripped the keys out of the ignition, then ran up the walkway to the old inn, taking the porch steps two at a time. Pebbles continued to bark insistently. Zoe tried the doorknob, but it didn't turn.

She held a hand over her eyes to peer through the dirt-smudged panes of the front window. Behind the glass, Pebbles whined and raced backward into the room. Zoe followed him with her eyes – all the way to a body lying prone on the rug in front of the sofa.

Her chest tightened. Something had happened to Celia. She had to get in the house somehow.

Celia had once made an offhand remark about her spare key being inside a hide-a-key rock that was so realistic, she couldn't remember which one it was. Zoe took one last look through the window, then scanned the garden and walkway for a rock big enough to conceal a house key. A few were stacked up next to the steps, so she scrambled down and started flipping them over. The third one was lighter than the others and revealed a little door underneath that she quickly slid open.

She jiggled the key in the lock until the knob finally gave, then ducked inside and swung the door shut behind her so Pebbles couldn't escape. She crossed the entry hall to the living room in five long steps.

Celia was stretched out on the rug with her leg bent at an awkward angle, her body unmoving. A knot on the side of her head protruded through her thinning white hair.

Zoe sucked in her breath and sent up a silent prayer: *Please, please let her be alive.*

She fell to her knees and felt Celia's wrist for a pulse. It was there, but thready. Celia didn't respond to her touch. Zoe nudged her shoulder gently, but didn't dare try to move her.

She yanked the phone out of her jacket pocket and dialed 911. "It's my neighbor. I think she must have fallen and hit her head. She's breathing, but not responding to anything." Zoe relayed the address and other necessary information to the operator, who gave her instructions to not move Celia and to stay with her until help arrived.

Like I would leave her alone like this. Zoe sat back against the front of the couch, her fingers resting lightly on Celia's hand as if she could keep her alive with that small contact. Pebbles lay on the floor near Celia, resting his head on his paws to stare mournfully at his mistress.

When the paramedics arrived, they took Celia's vitals and quickly assessed her injuries. "There's a possible cranial contusion, and her hip may be fractured," said a female EMT, who looked to be in her forties. The younger, male paramedic with her nodded, and they worked together to ease Celia into a scoop stretcher to take her to the ambulance.

"We're taking her to the county hospital," the man said. "You can meet us there."

Zoe nodded. "I'll be right behind you." She watched them slam the back doors of the ambulance, then closed her eyes for a moment. *Please let her be okay.*

She quickly said goodbye to Pebbles and locked the front door. As she got into her car, sirens screamed as the ambulance roared down the driveway, the driver swerving to avoid as many potholes as possible. When they reached the main road, they sped off, and Zoe followed as quickly as she dared to drive. When she reached the hospital, they were still in the process of getting Celia checked in.

"Are you Ms. James's emergency contact?" The woman behind the emergency room registration desk asked.

Zoe shook her head. "No. I rent a cottage from her, and I'm the one who found her." She choked back tears. "I don't know who to contact." The noise of the waiting room seemed to close in on her like she'd been dropped into a hive of angry bees. "Is she okay? Can I see her?"

"We're taking good care of her, and we'll let you know as soon as we have some information. Does Ms. James have any relatives?" The woman held out a clipboard with a thick stack of papers on it, the glittering, multicolored rings on her fingers a stark contrast to the harsh lighting and sterile, cream-colored walls.

Zoe took the clipboard without thinking and glanced at the first page which asked for the patient's name, address, insurance, allergies, etc. She could manage the name and address, but beyond that, she was clueless.

"I don't know if she has relatives." The realization stunned her. How had she lived next door to Celia for so long without finding out such a key piece of information?

The woman gave her a sympathetic look. "Let's have you fill out what you can of the paperwork. That'll give you some time to think about who to call."

Zoe eyed the forms again. "I'll try."

The woman's question about relatives ping-ponged in Zoe's brain as she filled out what she knew about Celia – which wasn't much. Celia's closest friend was Elizabeth Arnold, Meg's grandmother. Maybe she'd have a better idea of who to contact.

She turned in the forms to the woman behind the counter and dialed Meg.

"Hey, Zoe, what's up?" Meg sounded out of breath. "I just got back from a run. It's so gorgeous out tonight. All of the trees are getting their leaves back, and it's so green everywhere."

"Um." Zoe paused. "I'm actually calling because something happened to Celia."

There was silence on the other end of the line, then Meg said in a quiet voice, "Is ... is she okay?"

"I don't know yet. I found her on her living room floor when I came home from work." Zoe remembered the terror she'd felt at that moment, and her lip quivered. "She was breathing, but unconscious. I'm at the hospital now."

"Oh no." Meg's next words came out in a rush. "Is there anything I can do? Do you want me to come to the hospital and wait with you?"

Zoe considered Meg's offer. It had been a pretty horrible day, and although Meg was one of her best friends, she didn't think she could face talking to anyone yet about what had happened at work. "I think I'm okay here. I'll call you if I change my mind. But I was hoping to get your grandmother's phone number from you. When I was filling out Celia's intake forms, I realized I didn't have any clue who to call in an emergency."

"Of course. Let me pull it up." Meg was quiet for a moment, then she rattled off the ten-digit phone number. "Nana Elizabeth is in Arizona right now, though, so I'm not sure how much help she'll be."

Zoe's heart sank. She'd forgotten Elizabeth and her husband were snowbirds who escaped to Arizona every winter. "Well, maybe she'll at least be able to tell me if there's someone I should notify."

"I hope so. You know, I never thought about it before either, but Celia's never talked much about anything personal. She's always quick to comfort any of us, but I don't know much about her life, other than she's lived at the old Inn for as long as I can remember." Meg's voice cracked. "I wish now that I'd thought to ask her."

"Me too." Zoe sighed. It wasn't something she could change at this point. "I'm going to give your grandmother a call and see if she can help."

"Let me know if you change your mind about me coming to the hospital. I'll let my family and Cassie know, too, but we'll wait for you to let us know if it's okay to come."

"Thanks." A tear dripped down Zoe's cheek, and she swiped at it with the back of her hand. "I'll call when I know something."

She hung up and immediately dialed Elizabeth Arnold.

"Hello?" A woman answered brightly.

"Mrs. Arnold? It's Zoe Tisdale, Meg's friend in Willa Bay."

"Oh yes, Zoe." Her demeanor changed, and concern tinged her words. "Is everything okay with Meg? Or the other girls?"

"Yes, they're fine. I'm calling about Celia." She hurried to add, "She's alive, but in the hospital."

"Oh goodness. What happened? Is she okay?"

Zoe took a deep breath. "It looked like she fell at home. I found her unconscious and called an ambulance. I'm at the ER, but they haven't let me see her yet."

"So, you don't know anything?" Elizabeth asked. Her voice was muffled as she told someone next to her that Celia was in the hospital.

"No. Nothing yet."

"Well, she's alive. That's something."

"The thing is, I'm not sure who to notify. They want to know her emergency contact. If she makes it—" Zoe choked on the words. "The paramedics thought her leg looked broken, so she may need surgery. There will be decisions to make."

"Oh."

Elizabeth was silent for so long that Zoe said, "Hello? Are you still there?"

"I'm still here." Elizabeth sighed. "You know Celia's a very private person, right?"

"Right." Where was Elizabeth going with this?

"I don't know if I should tell you this, but I think Celia would want him to know."

Him? "I'm sorry, who?" Zoe asked.

"Look in the old sewing desk. She keeps her address book there. Call Shawn."

"Do you know his last name?" Zoe had never heard Celia mention a Shawn before.

"Sorry, honey. That's all I know." She uttered a long sigh. "I hope I don't regret this."

"Who is this Shawn guy?" Zoe asked.

"I can't say. If ... *When* Celia wakes up, she can tell you." Elizabeth sighed again. "Just call him and tell him that Celia's in the hospital, and he's her emergency contact."

"Okay." Zoe was intensely curious, but she didn't think Elizabeth was going to divulge any further information about the man. "I'll go to her house and call him. Thanks, Elizabeth."

"Of course. And Zoe? Please let me know as soon as you have any news about Celia. She's been a dear friend of mine for as long as I can remember."

"I will." Zoe ended the call and walked over to the front desk. There were two people in front of her: a man with blood dripping from his thumb, and a woman wearing a face mask. When it was her turn, she approached the woman behind the desk. "Do you have any update on Celia James?"

The woman shook her head. "I'm sorry, we don't know anything yet. Have a seat and we'll let you know when we do. Did you find her emergency contact yet?"

"I need to go home and find her address book." Zoe glanced at the full waiting room. "I should be back in about an hour and half, but if there's news about Celia, can you please call me?"

"I can do that." The woman pulled up Celia's chart and noted Zoe's phone number. "Drive carefully, please. We don't want to see you arrive in an ambulance too."

Zoe managed a wan smile. "I will. Thank you." She walked out of the ER, then broke into a jog as she crossed the parking lot to her car. Remembering the woman's advice, she drove the speed limit all the way back to Celia's house.

The spare key was still in her jeans pocket. When she opened the door, Pebbles was waiting in the entry hall. He tried to nose past her, seeking his mistress. Zoe's heart broke.

"Sorry, Pebbles." She stroked his coarse fur, but he kept looking around as if Celia was hiding behind her. "Your mama will be home soon." *I hope.*

Breathe, Zoe, she reminded herself. She was there on a mission. She needed to find Shawn's phone number quickly and get back to the hospital.

She petted Pebbles again, then went into the living room, studiously averting her eyes from the spot on the floor where Celia had lain earlier. She pulled on the center drawer of the antique sewing table, but it didn't budge. With some coaxing, it finally creaked open, revealing a thin local phone book and Celia's address book.

She flipped through the pages, which, judging by the volume of crossed out addresses and phone numbers, had been used for at least the last thirty years. She'd be lucky to find Shawn's phone number in all of this mess.

Pebbles nudged her leg, and when she looked down to pet him, Shawn's name jumped off the page. *Found it.*

There was nothing special about how Celia had noted his name – nothing to indicate how she knew him. But Elizabeth had told her that he was Celia's emergency contact. The area code was for the region of Washington State just south of Seattle. Zoe dialed his number and waited. It rang six times before he answered.

"Hello?" The man's voice was thick with sleep, but younger than she'd expected.

"Hi. May I speak with Shawn Curtin please?" Zoe asked.

"This is Shawn." His voice had become clearer, but more guarded.

"I'm sorry to bother you, but I'm calling about Celia James." She waited for his response.

"Who?"

Well, she hadn't expected *that*.

"Celia James. I'm calling from Willa Bay, Washington. This *is* Shawn Curtin, right?"

"Yes, but I don't know a Celia James." Zoe heard a rhythmic noise on the other end of the line, as though he were tapping his finger or a pen against something while he tried to think. "Wait. Maybe I do. You're calling from Washington, right?"

She nodded, then realized he couldn't see what she was doing. "Yes. Celia is my neighbor here in Willa Bay. She's had an accident and is in the hospital. You're listed as her emergency contact."

Shawn exhaled loudly. "What?"

This was definitely not going to plan, not that she'd had one in mind. "Celia has you listed as her emergency contact."

"Why would she do that?" His voice was deep, with just a hint of a southern drawl.

"I have no idea." Zoe was starting to wonder if Celia was in the Witness Protection program or something. How was her emergency contact so clueless about who she was? "Look, she's in the hospital. Last I heard, she was unconscious and may need surgery for her leg. Can you just come up to Willa Bay and talk to the doctors? I can't make any decisions for her because I'm not family."

"Well, neither am I. At least not close family." He sighed. "There's not much I can do out here in Charleston."

"Like Charleston, South Carolina?" This was getting more confusing by the second. Celia's emergency contact didn't know her and lived on the other side of the country. "You aren't in Washington State?"

"Nope." There was the southern twang again.

"Oh." She didn't know what to say. She couldn't expect him to fly cross-country on a moment's notice. Now what?

"Look, I'll see what I can do. I'm not sure when I can catch the next flight out to Seattle." He cleared his throat. "It's late here. How about I call you tomorrow morning, and we can work out a plan? Maybe this Celia woman will be awake by then and can make her own decisions."

"Okay." There wasn't much more she could do, and he had a point – Celia could wake up at any time. "I'll talk to you tomorrow." Her phone beeped to alert her to another call. "I've got to go."

"Talk to you tomorrow." The call with Shawn dropped and the other call picked up.

"Hello, I'm calling from the Skamish County Hospital," said a woman's perky voice. "I'm looking for Zoe Tisdale."

"I'm Zoe." She steeled herself for bad news.

"Ms. Tisdale, I wanted to let you know that we have Mrs. James stabilized, and she'll be undergoing surgery tomorrow morning at six o'clock."

Zoe let out the breath she'd been holding and flopped down on the sofa. "So, she's awake?"

The woman sighed. "No ma'am. She's still unconscious, but her vitals are stable."

"Should I come back to the hospital? I just came home to grab a few things and to call her emergency contact."

"I'm sorry. She's in the intensive care unit right now, so she's not allowed any visitors. You're welcome to wait in the surgical waiting room tomorrow morning, but I suggest you get some rest now."

"I will. Thank you." The phone clicked and Zoe hung up, staring aimlessly at Celia's living room. Pebbles jumped up on the couch with her and snuggled close.

Rest. Like that was even possible. This had been one of

the worst days of her life, and tomorrow didn't promise to be any better. It was going to kill her to see Pearson training with Joan.

But that didn't matter right now. She planned to be at the hospital early tomorrow morning in case Celia woke up. At least she'd have a good excuse for not going in to work.

Zoe put Pebbles on a leash and took him outside for a quick potty break, then located some food for him in the kitchen before she left for home. She changed into pajamas and tried to read the book she was in the middle of, but her ability to concentrate was shot. She eventually gave up and fell into a fitful sleep.

6

Shawn

After Zoe hung up the phone, Shawn sat up and stared at the alarm clock on the floor next to his mattress. A quarter to midnight. When the phone rang, he'd answered immediately, conditioned by years of late-night phone calls from his direct reports while he was a sergeant in the Army. The habit hadn't died, even after retirement.

This was one of the oddest calls he'd ever received, though, ranking up there with the one he'd received in the middle of the night from a frantic group of drunk corporals who'd accidentally released a prize bull from its pasture. Who was Celia James, and why did she have him down as her emergency contact?

He turned on his bedside lamp and glanced at the framed photo of his parents that rested on the top of one of two sets of plastic drawers in the room. His eyes skimmed over the image of his dad and landed on his mother. She'd lost her battle with cancer eight years ago, and he still missed her every day. He knew his dad did too.

Shawn had only seen Jack and Andrea Curtin argue seriously once in his life, when he was about ten years old. He'd been awoken from a deep sleep by their raised voices and crept out of bed to hide in the hallway, just out of sight. The incident had left an impression on him that he remembered as clearly as if it had happened yesterday.

"No!" his normally meek mother had shouted. "I don't want anything to do with Celia. She's not a part of my life and never will be."

"She wants to be a part of your life though. She's family, Andrea." His father's voice was calm, but firm.

"No. She gave up that right a long time ago." She'd added something in a quieter voice.

Shawn had poked his head out to hear better, which caught his father's attention.

"Shawn," his father had said. "Come out here."

He'd never forget the tears on his mother's cheeks as he crept forward and stood awkwardly in the doorway to the living room. She'd looked straight at him, then covered her face and walked out of the room.

"She's okay," his father told him. "Don't worry, son."

"Why is Mom crying?"

His father had started to say something but then thought better of it. "It's a family thing. Maybe she'll tell you when you're older. For now, let's get you back to bed." He led Shawn back to his room and kissed his forehead. "Everything's okay. Don't worry."

By morning, his mom was fine, making pancakes and eggs for breakfast like nothing had happened. A few weeks later, Shawn asked his dad about Celia, and his dad had brushed him off, saying she was his mom's aunt, but not to mention her. Out of deference to his mom, he'd never brought the subject up again. Now he wished he had.

His mom wasn't around to answer the questions that burned in his mind, but maybe his dad could. He checked the clock again and mentally calculated the time difference. Not too late to call. Jack Curtin still lived in Tacoma, about thirty miles south of Seattle, in a house he'd bought while stationed at the Army post known at that time as Fort Lewis.

The phone rang a few times and then went to voicemail, his dad's familiar voice telling him to leave a message. Too late, Shawn recalled his dad mentioning a planned trip to his fishing cabin in the Cascade Mountains. Shawn ended the call without saying anything.

He set the phone down on the floor and eyed the room's spartan furnishings. He'd fallen in love with Charleston while stationed nearby, and when he'd retired last year, he'd purchased a run-down house in the historic district to remodel. He'd completed the renovations last week and put the property on the market. It had sold within a day and was scheduled to close in only a few weeks.

Shawn had planned to stick around and buy another fixer-upper, but he needed the sales proceeds from the current place first. Until then, he was stuck in limbo, waiting around until he could get started on his next project. Fully awake now, he paced mindlessly through every room in the house, thinking about the mysterious phone call. Who was Celia? Should he fly to Seattle to find out?

He didn't have many belongings to pack, and the house was ready for its new owners. He'd identified a few prospects for his next project but hadn't yet made any offers. There was nothing concrete keeping him in Charleston.

Shawn's thoughts cleared as he walked to the granite-topped island he'd installed in the center of the kitchen. He opened his laptop, clicked on the icon for his Internet browser, and navigated to his favorite travel website.

He would go to Seattle to finally solve the mystery of his long unanswered question. Even if Celia recovered and didn't need him, he'd be near home and could see his dad. It had been a while, and this would be the perfect time for a visit.

7

CASSIE

Cassie crossed the Lodge's kitchen and removed a trio of cakes from the oven, setting them on a rack to cool. They were perfectly golden on top, although with all the chocolate frosting she planned to use, no one would ever see their perfection. She loved that aspect of cake decorating; what the cakes actually looked like under all the frosting was her little secret. As long as the final product tasted great and exceeded the client's expectations, nothing else mattered.

There was always plenty to do when she arrived at the Lodge early in the morning. The restaurant was closed during the first part of the week, but every morning they provided an array of baked goods for breakfast. When that ended an hour ago, she'd immediately switched over to preparations for the next day's desserts. The cakes were a new recipe she was testing for a wedding at the end of the month and she'd frost them later.

She eyed the clock on the wall, surprised to see it was

already eleven. She had twenty minutes until she needed to leave to pick up Jace at school for his appointment at the Seattle Autism Center. Her stomach churned like she'd just eaten three huge pieces of chocolate cake. Today was the day they'd find out if Jace qualified for an autism diagnosis. While the idea that her son could be autistic was a little scary, it would provide answers – and hopefully some tools to help him cope as he got older and his teachers expected more from him.

Before leaving, Cassie checked to make sure there were chocolate chip cookies at the front desk, but all that remained on the silver platter were a few crumbs. The cookie recipe was one that she'd tweaked for years before she was satisfied with it, and they were a hit with guests. She grabbed the platter off the tall counter near the front desk and took it back to the kitchen to refill it.

As she walked back to the kitchen, she stopped to knock on Zoe's closed office door. There was no answer, and the light was off. It wasn't like Zoe to not come in to work. Meg had called last night to tell Cassie about Celia's accident, but she hadn't heard anything since then.

Worry gnawed at Cassie as she placed cookies on the platter and brought them back to the front desk. As soon as she was back in the kitchen, she called Zoe. Her friend didn't answer. She thought about calling Meg to see if she'd heard any news about Celia, but if Cassie didn't leave immediately, she'd be late picking up Jace.

He was still packing up his stuff when Cassie arrived at the school. She tried to be patient while waiting for him to finish getting ready and out to the car, but she couldn't help worrying about the ticking clock. After battling traffic all the way to Seattle, Cassie finally pulled into a parking spot at the Autism Center and looked at Jace in the rearview mirror. "Honey, we're here."

Jace continued playing on his tablet.

"Hey." She twisted in her seat to face him. "We're here. It's time to go to your appointment."

He looked up briefly, then returned to his game.

"Jace. We have to go."

He sighed loudly. "Fine."

They got out of the car and checked in for the appointment. Jace immediately settled in with his tablet, but Cassie's nerves were on fire. *I wish Kyle were here.* The thought surprised her. Kyle had never taken an active role in parenting, and he'd opposed her desire to have Jace evaluated for autism. Still, it would have been nice to have another adult present.

"Jace Randolph?" A woman called out from the other side of the waiting room.

Cassie stood, and pulled Jace to a standing position. "Jace, that's you." She led him up to the woman.

The woman smiled at him. "It's nice to meet you, Jace. I'm Mary."

He gave Mary a wary look but didn't say anything.

As they followed Mary back into the depths of the clinic, Mary explained that she was a psychiatric nurse practitioner and would be working with a psychiatrist to evaluate Jace. She asked Cassie a bunch of questions, then spoke individually to Jace.

The next few hours were a blur until the evaluation was complete, and Cassie once again found herself sitting across a desk from Mary while Jace played with Legos in the corner.

Mary folded her hands in front of her on the desk. "So, I've met with the psychiatrist and we've discussed both the behavior you've noted in Jace and what we've seen today. Based on the criteria we use to diagnose autism in a child, Jace does fall on the autism spectrum."

Cassie's heart stopped. She'd both hoped for and dreaded the diagnosis, but to hear it for real was more emotional than she'd expected. Her eyes blurred, and Mary handed her a tissue.

"I'm sorry," Cassie blurted out as she dabbed at her eyes. "It's just a lot to take in."

"There's no need to apologize," Mary said.

Cassie took a few breaths to calm her nerves. "You always hear that you'll know if your kid has autism when they're a baby because they won't make eye contact, or around two years old because they start losing words. Jace never had those issues."

Mary gave her a placid smile. She'd probably heard this from parents many times before. "Lack of eye contact and speech regression are two of the signs we look for, but there are other things too."

Cassie nodded. "It's a bit of a shock to discover it at this age." She quickly added, "I'm not upset about it, just processing." She looked over at Jace, who didn't appear to have heard any of the exchange between his mother and the nurse.

"Of course. I understand." Mary reached for some brochures and handed them to Cassie. "This is a description of some of the classes we offer for parents." She gave Cassie a list of resources and told her about some types of therapies that might help Jace. "I'll be sending you a report of our findings. Do you have any other questions?"

Cassie stared at her. She had so many questions that she didn't know what to ask first. It was at times like this that she really wished her parents lived closer – or that Kyle was there with her. She gestured to the brochures. "I think I'll start with these."

"Good idea." Mary smiled softly at her. "It can be kind

of overwhelming at first. If you think of questions later, feel free to give us a call."

"I will." Cassie went to Jace and tapped him on the shoulder. He didn't react, so she gently tugged at his arm. He protested, but finally gave in.

"Are we done?" he asked.

"Yep. We're done with the clinic." *For today,* she thought. There was a long journey ahead of them, and she didn't know how Kyle would react to Jace's diagnosis.

After their day at the clinic, she took Jace for a cheeseburger and a milkshake. As she watched him chow down on his food, she was overcome with love for him. He and Amanda were everything to her, and she'd do anything for them. Nothing would change that. If anything, having the autism diagnosis would help Jace get the assistance he needed to succeed not just in school and, later, in life.

~

Cassie had asked Kyle to come over after the kids were in bed so they could discuss Jace's appointment. Even after having him out of the house for two years, it felt weird to see him on the front porch, knocking on the door as though he were a stranger.

She opened the door. "Hi."

"Are the kids asleep?" he asked.

She shook her head. "I think Jace probably is, but Amanda's still reading. I think we can talk in the kitchen, though, without her hearing."

He nodded and followed her into the kitchen.

"Do you want some coffee?" she asked, gesturing to the coffeemaker. "I just made a fresh pot of decaf." From years of marriage, she knew Kyle always drank a cup or two of decaf in the evening.

He smiled at her gratefully. "That would be great. I came straight here after work. I haven't even been home for dinner."

"Ah, tax season. I don't miss that." She grinned at him. When she wasn't irritated with him, she could almost remember what it was like to sit down with him in the evenings and share a pot of coffee after the kids were asleep.

"Almost done. I can't wait." He rolled his eyes. "I swear, every year I tell my clients to get their tax info in to me as soon as they receive it, but they always wait until the last minute." Cassie handed him a mug. He took a small sip and set it down. "So, Jace's appointment. How did it go?"

She set her own coffee on the kitchen table and sat down across from him. "They said he fits the criteria for an autism diagnosis."

He looked down into his mug, then back up at her. "Are they sure?"

"As sure as they can be." She shrugged. "There's criteria, but I think a lot of it is their impression of him. There are things that he does and says that are common for kids with autism."

Kyle shook his head. "No. Jace doesn't have autism. He's just a quirky kid."

Cassie pressed her lips together. She'd known this wasn't going to be easy. "This hasn't changed anything about him."

"I know. Because he doesn't have autism." He raised his jaw and locked eyes with her.

She sighed. "Whether you believe it or not, this is a good thing. Now our insurance will pay for some of the occupational and behavioral therapies for him."

"How much is that going to cost me?" he grumbled.

Cassie would have been angry with his reaction, but she saw the tears glistening in his eyes. This wasn't easy for him to accept.

"I need to look into it, but we'll figure it out. I need to find out if there are some accommodations that the school can make to help him learn too."

"He's a smart kid. Why does he need accommodations?" Kyle asked.

She mentally counted to three before responding, but she couldn't keep the snarkiness out of her words. "He *is* smart, but he has trouble keeping up with the other kids because things move so fast. If you'd ever attended any of his parent-teacher conferences, you'd know he's struggling at school."

Kyle's spine stiffened. "I have a job I have to be at during the day."

"So do I, but I make the time." She stared back at him, not backing down. He looked out the window, then back at her. She held her breath, wondering what he'd say.

His eyes closed briefly, then opened as he nodded at her, seeming to recognize for the first time everything she did. "That you do. So, what do *we* do now?"

She stood, picking up the stack of brochures Mary had given her from where she'd set them on the counter, and laid them out in front of her ex-husband. "Now *we* move forward."

8

Zoe

Zoe got to the hospital early Tuesday morning and settled into a chair in the surgical waiting room with a book and a traveler mug of coffee. She'd hoped to see Celia before she went into surgery, but the nurse in charge told her Celia was still unconscious and unable to receive visitors before her surgery. Zoe was so on edge that even a book by her favorite author wasn't able to distract her from worrying about everything going on in her life.

It was too early to call Joan yet to let her know she wouldn't be in to work, so that unsavory task hung over her. The nurse said they should have some news about Celia's condition in about four hours. Shawn Curtin hadn't called her back, but after the disastrous phone call the night before, she wouldn't be surprised if he never did. She wasn't sure what that meant in terms of Celia's care.

With Celia's accident and everything going on at work, Zoe felt like her carefully planned life had been tossed into chaotic and unknown territory, and all she could do was to wait and see how things turned out.

At eight o'clock, she got up from her seat and walked

down to the cafeteria, where the cell phone reception was better. When she called Joan, the phone rang several times, but there was no answer. Zoe left a short message stating she wouldn't be in that day and hung up, then returned to the waiting room. It would have been better to talk to Joan in person, but by now, Joan must know that Zoe had been passed over for the promotion. It was a relief to not have to discuss it with her right then.

A few more hours passed, and a middle-aged man dressed in blue scrubs came through the swinging doors from the OR. "Zoe Tisdale?" His eyes searched the room.

She held her hand in the air as she stood. "I'm Zoe." She took a few steps forward, trying to judge Celia's condition from his demeanor, but his face was poker-straight and didn't give her much to go on. Chills ran up her spine. Was Celia okay?

When she neared him, he said, "I'm Dr. Fyfe. We just finished Mrs. James's surgery, and she'll be heading to recovery soon."

She breathed a sigh of relief. If nothing else, Celia was still alive. "Thank you."

He smiled at her, but it didn't quite reach his eyes. "She did well in surgery, but she's not out of the woods yet. She appears to have hit her head pretty hard when she fell, and she's still in a coma."

Zoe stared at her shoes, then looked back up at him. "Do you know when she might come out of it?"

He shook his head. "The brain is a tricky thing. It could be hours, or it could be days or months." His voice became gentler. "You need to know that there's also the possibility that she may never awaken."

Zoe bit her upper lip to hold back tears. "How likely is that?"

"We really don't know. Only time will tell." He glanced

back at the swinging doors. "I'd better get back, but if you have any more questions, please don't hesitate to ask the doctors in charge of Mrs. James's care. You should be able to see her in about two hours when they have her settled in a room. Now would be a great time to grab some lunch or something."

Zoe nodded. "Thank you. I appreciate you taking the time to let me know how she's doing." Her lip quivered. "I feel so helpless."

He awkwardly patted her on the shoulder. "It's normal to feel that way. Mrs. James is lucky to have you in her corner though." He turned and strode back through the doors.

Zoe collected her belongings and went home to check on Pebbles. He was happy to see her but still searching for his mistress. She put him on a leash and took him for a walk. Pebbles bounced eagerly down the rickety stairs to the beach and immediately nosed at every rock, stick, and piece of seaweed he could find.

She watched the dog roaming the beach, the leash extended as far as it could go. Everything seemed new to him, which made sense because it would have been difficult for Celia to navigate the stairs to the beach. While he played, she took the time to really look at the inn.

It must have been beautiful when it was open. She knew Celia couldn't handle running it as an inn anymore, but it was a shame for such a gorgeous place to not be shared with more people. Zoe knew she was lucky to have the opportunity to live on the grounds.

She spotted her cottage, barely visible from where she sat on a beach log. Even if she woke up soon, Celia would likely need to stay in a rehabilitation center as she recovered from her broken leg and hip. What would that mean for the Inn – or for Zoe's cottage? Would she have to move?

Her stomach churned. The thought was selfish, but she couldn't help it. It was sour icing on a rotten cake to be faced with losing not only a long-awaited promotion, but possibly also her home and a good friend, all at the same time.

Pebbles barked, breaking Zoe away from her mental spiral. She stood and breathed in the salty air. Worrying wasn't helping anything. "What's up, boy?" She walked closer to where he stood, fixated on something in the trees.

She followed his gaze. A squirrel leapt from one branch to another in a tall maple tree, sending a leaf floating to the ground. Pebbles barked again and tugged at the leash.

Zoe laughed. "Sorry, buddy." She glanced at her watch. There was just enough time before Celia was allowed visitors for Zoe to get Pebbles back, grab a sandwich at her cottage, and head back to the hospital.

As she filled Pebbles's water bowl and gave him some food, her phone beeped to let her know she'd received a text message.

My flight arrives at six tonight. I'll give you a call when I get to the hospital. ~ Shawn

She re-read the text, unconvinced that she'd read it correctly the first time. He was actually coming. Zoe knew almost nothing about the man, but somehow the thought that he'd arrive soon was comforting. At least she wouldn't be alone in making decisions about Celia's welfare.

～

The elevator ride to the seventh floor seemed interminably long. Zoe watched as the numbers flashed by, hardly noticing the other passengers as they got on and off. When the indicator light finally reached the number seven and the doors opened, she stepped out into the hallway and scanned the room numbers next to each door to get her bearings. It looked like room 732 was just a few doors down from the elevator lobby.

Zoe walked along the speckled vinyl floors, stopping in front of Celia's room. The door was ajar, and the room was quiet. It didn't appear as though any doctors or nurses were in there with her. A rustling noise behind her caught her attention, and she turned to see a woman wearing dark purple scrubs standing behind her. An ID tag hung from a lanyard around her neck, but Zoe couldn't quite make out her name.

"Did you need any help?" the woman asked.

Zoe's eyes darted to Celia's room. "I was hoping to visit Celia James. I believe this is her room?"

The woman smiled at her. "You've got the right place. The doctor just left. Are you family?"

"I'm probably the closest thing to family she has," Zoe said.

"Well, the doctor will be by soon, and you'll have a chance to talk to him then."

Zoe smiled at her gratefully. "Thank you. Is it okay if I go in?"

"Sure, go ahead. She hasn't woken up yet, but I personally feel like it's good for people to talk to their loved ones who are in a coma. I think they know when people are around them."

Zoe entered Celia's room and stopped about five feet away from the bed. A strong odor of antiseptic pervaded every space in the hospital, including this one. Other than that, though, it was a comfortable single room with a sleeper sofa and a large picture window overlooking the farmlands behind the campus.

She moved closer. Celia lay under a mound of blankets, her petite figure seeming smaller and more fragile than usual. Her fluffy white hair and pale skin blended in with the starched pillowcase.

Zoe opened the two folding chairs that had been stacked against the wall and placed them next to the bed. She put her purse on one and sat on the other, reaching for Celia's hand. The elderly woman's wrinkled fingers were chilly on the outside of the blanket. Zoe wasn't sure if she was hoping for a miracle, but Celia didn't respond when Zoe squeezed her hand.

What should she say to her? Was the nurse correct about comatose patients being able to hear? If so, Celia didn't need to hear about Zoe's lost promotion. That kind of bad news could wait until Celia woke up and was healthy again.

She gazed at the older woman's face. Celia's breath came out of her pale lips in little puffs of air as Zoe launched into a tale about a particularly obnoxious bride-to-be. It was probably her imagination, but it made Zoe feel better to think that she'd seen the corners of Celia's lips turn up at the funniest part of the story.

When she finished, she got up and walked to the window. "Hey, Celia, you've got a great view from here. I can even see the tulip fields. I know how much you love the tulips. You'll have to wake up soon or you'll miss seeing them bloom."

It felt weird to be talking to someone who didn't react. She glanced at her watch. It was one o'clock. Shawn wasn't due to arrive for over five more hours.

Zoe picked up her tablet and tried to get back into the

e-book she'd been reading. She was a few pages in when the door opened, and a short man wearing a long white coat over light-blue scrubs entered the room.

He consulted his clipboard, then held out his hand. "Hello, I'm Doctor Maize. Are you Zoe Tisdale?"

She nodded. "Yes."

"Great. One of my colleagues notified me that there was someone here visiting Mrs. James, and I thought I'd check in with you."

She wasn't sure whether she should stay seated or get up. She opted to turn her chair sideways so she could face him, but still remain close to Celia's side.

The doctor moved to the other side of Celia's bed and quickly took stock of all of the monitors. He nodded and made a note on his clipboard. "It looks like Mrs. James is recovering nicely from her surgery."

"Do you know when she might wake up?" Zoe asked.

He smiled sadly at her and shook his head. "No, I'm sorry. These things aren't terribly predictable."

Her heart sank. It was the same thing the surgeon had told her earlier.

"So, she might be here for weeks or months?"

"We aren't sure at this point, but as soon as she's in a stable condition and able to be released, we can move her to a rehabilitation facility where she'll be more comfortable. Even if she wakes up, she'll need time to recuperate from her surgery."

"Oh." Zoe's mind raced. She didn't know anything about Celia's insurance or what it would cover.

He held up his hand. "I know you're probably worrying about what comes next, but let's just take it one step at a time. Okay?"

She sighed and nodded her head. Maybe Shawn would have some answers about Celia's insurance. From what he'd said last night, though, she seriously doubted he had any sort of relationship with Celia and most likely wouldn't be much help.

The doctor eyed the door, but smiled at her kindly. "Did you have any other questions for me?"

Questions? She had hundreds, but she needed to get some information from Shawn before she proceeded. "I don't have any right now, but I'm sure I will have plenty later."

He nodded briskly. "I'll be back in about two hours to check on her, and, of course, the nurses will be keeping an eye on her as well. If you need anything, please don't hesitate to ask."

"Thank you. I will."

He hustled out of the room, the tails of his jacket billowing out behind him with each stride. She was alone again with her thoughts.

"Did you hear that, Celia? I'm hoping you're going to wake up soon, but until you do, I'll make sure they take good care of you."

Celia's chest rose up and down rhythmically, and her monitors didn't reflect any reaction to her or the doctor talking. She forced her attention back to her book. The hours ticked by slowly, but she was still surprised when her phone rang with a number that looked familiar.

"Zoe? It's Shawn Curtin. My flight just landed in Seattle, but I realized that we never made any firm plans for when I arrived.

"Oh. Hi. I was wondering when you'd call," she stammered. Something about him unnerved her, but he didn't seem to notice.

"I'm planning on catching the airport shuttle up to Willa Bay, but should I come directly to the hospital, or is there a different location that would be better?"

She checked her watch. It was rush hour and Seattle's freeways would be clogged and unpredictable. "How about you meet me at the hospital. I'm in Celia's room – room seven-three-two. When you get here, you can visit with her, and we can make a plan for her care."

"Visit with her? Does that mean she's awake now?" Excitement tinged his voice.

Her heart stopped for a moment. "Oh, I'm so sorry." It hadn't been her intention to get his hopes up. "No, she's still not awake. Surgery went well though."

"Oh. Good to hear that," he said, then added quickly, "The surgery part, not the other."

She chuckled. "I knew what you meant. It should take you about two or three hours to get up here, so I might step out and get a bite for dinner. I won't leave the hospital, though, so just give me a call if I'm not here."

She heard people shuffling around him.

"Looks like we're unloading now, so I'd better get going. See you soon."

"You too." They hung up, and Zoe studied the older woman, once again wondering about her mysterious connection with Shawn. It felt a little intrusive to meet a relative of an incapacitated person, but at this point Zoe didn't really have any other choice.

~

Zoe finished eating the dry turkey sandwich from the cafeteria that she'd brought back to Celia's room and washed it down with a swig of Diet Coke. She stood to throw the wrapper away and heard footsteps outside the door. It was time for the nurse to check in on Celia, so Zoe threw her garbage in the can without looking at the door.

However, instead of the nurse, it was a man who

appeared to be in his late thirties, with close-cropped, dark-brown hair. He was tall, probably close to six feet, and wore a navy-blue zip-up jacket over well-worn denim jeans.

He eyed the bed but didn't approach Celia immediately. "Is this Celia James's room?" His words held a hint of a Southern drawl that she found intriguing.

"Yes, this is Celia's room." She peered at him. Was this Shawn? And if so, why didn't he recognize Celia?

He walked toward her, limping slightly, and held out his hand. "I'm Shawn Curtin."

Zoe shook it. "Zoe Tisdale. Nice to meet you."

He stuck his hands in his jacket pockets and crossed over to stand about a foot away from Celia's bed. "And this is Celia, I presume?"

Zoe watched him carefully. There was no tenderness in his expression, only clinical detachment like he was trying to place Celia. "Yes. How long has it been since you last saw each other?"

He continued scrutinizing the elderly woman's face, then turned to Zoe. "As far as I know, we've never met."

Zoe stepped back. "Never?" How was that even possible? Why would Celia have listed him as her emergency contact if they'd never met?

He shrugged. "Nope."

"Okay ..." she said slowly. "Then how are you related?"

His eyes locked with hers. "Honestly, I have no idea if we are even related."

She closed her eyes for a moment. Shawn wasn't going to be much help with Celia's personal affairs. Who was this guy? And why hadn't Elizabeth told her that Shawn didn't know Celia?

"So, you flew out here to see an unconscious woman

whom you'd never met before?" She looked between him and Celia, hoping to see a familial resemblance.

He shrugged again and shuffled his feet. "It sounded like it was important for me to be here." He paused for a moment. "I think we're related somehow. I once heard my parents arguing about someone named Celia, but they never mentioned her again. I've always been curious about her identity." He moved even closer to the hospital bed and gestured to Celia. "If I'm listed as this woman's emergency contact, I'm going to connect the dots here and say my parents were talking about her."

Zoe wasn't sure what to say. She took a deep breath, then let it out slowly. "Okay then. Let's try to get to the bottom of this."

"Sounds good to me." He looked around the room, as if noticing the flashing monitors for the first time. "Is there someone I should talk to?"

"The doctor just came by for his last round of the night. You can talk to him in the morning. Celia hasn't woken up since her fall, so I think we should let her rest. We can head to her house now to see if we can figure out why she listed you as her emergency contact." Zoe sensed that Elizabeth Arnold knew who Shawn was to Celia but didn't want to betray her friend's secrets, even in this situation. If she was going to tell Zoe about Shawn, she would have done so earlier. It was up to them to figure it out on their own.

Shawn hesitated. "I don't know how I feel about searching her house without her permission."

Zoe sighed and glanced at Celia. "I don't either, but we don't know when she'll wake up. It could be tomorrow or it could be next year. If we're going to make decisions for her, I'd like to have a good understanding of the situation."

He nodded. "I'll defer to you then."

Zoe said goodbye to Celia, and they left her room.

"I'm going to let the nurses know we'll be back tomorrow morning," Zoe said over her shoulder.

Shawn didn't say anything, but his footsteps were heavy behind hers as he followed her to the nurses station. Things weren't going according to plan at all, but she had a feeling that this was going to be an interesting evening.

9

Shawn

Shawn watched through the passenger side mirror as the hospital disappeared behind them. He'd hoped when he saw Celia for the first time that he would instantly recognize her, and the mystery would be solved. Unfortunately, no matter how hard he tried to remember her, she was still a stranger to him.

Although his mother had kept careful photo albums of him and his younger sister, Jessa, when they were kids, there were few pictures of his mother's family. He couldn't remember ever seeing a photo of the woman who lay in that hospital bed, even allowing for the passage of decades.

He turned away from the window and looked over at Zoe. "Do you have any recommendations for a hotel I can stay at?"

She took her attention away from the road to eye him with surprise. "Oh. I guess I assumed you'd stay at Celia's house. I hadn't really thought that far ahead." She glanced at the road and then back at him. "Is that okay with you? I don't think Celia would mind, and there are plenty of extra bedrooms."

He opened his mouth to speak, then stopped. For once in his life, he wasn't sure what to say. It felt odd to stay in a stranger's house while she was in the hospital. Would Celia want him to be there?

Zoe seemed to sense his discomfort. "It's not that late yet. How about we come back to this a little later?"

He nodded and returned his gaze to the window. "Is this Willa Bay here?"

"No, the hospital is in Skamish, but we'll be in Willa Bay soon." She drove along a four-lane highway for a few more minutes, then turned off onto a two-lane country road.

The sun was low in the sky but provided enough light to show off the tulip fields on either side of the road. The variety of colors almost took his breath away. Although he'd spent years of his life in Washington State before he'd enlisted in the Army, he'd never been to this part of it.

"I feel like I'm in Holland," he said. "I keep expecting to see windmills or something."

She laughed. "I hear that a lot." The tulips fields disappeared from sight and she turned down a street with cute shops lining both sides. "Actually, a lot of people in the US will order tulips from Holland, only to find out they were actually grown right here in Willa Bay." She pointed at the shops and the body of water behind them. "This is Main Street here, and that's the Willomish River."

"Is Celia's house close to town?" He wasn't sure what to expect from her place. Zoe had mentioned there being extra bedrooms, but maybe he'd be better off in a hotel than intruding on Celia's personal space.

"It's a bit out of town, but within walking distance." The row of stores ended, and Zoe turned left onto a street that bordered the bay. Shawn watched in amazement as they passed driveways so long that he couldn't even see the mansions he imagined were at the end of them.

Zoe left the main road, and the car jolted over terrain rough enough to make his teeth click together. He placed his hands on the dashboard to brace himself.

She eyed his outstretched arms and shot him an impish grin. "Sorry, this road badly needs to be re-graveled. You get used to it."

"Does Celia live off of this road?" He couldn't see anything but trees and brush.

"This is her driveway."

His jaw dropped, and he turned to stare at her. "Celia *owns* this?"

She nodded. A tall blue building came into view, and Zoe parked in front of the walkway that led up to it. Shawn's eyes were so wide now that he had to force himself to blink. "What is this place?"

"It's the old Inn at Willa Bay. Celia and her husband, Charlie, ran it until he died about ten years ago." She got out of the car and walked to the edge of the lawn, scanning the property with a wistful smile on her face. "It's seen better days, but it's still beautiful. I do wish I could have seen it when it was in full swing though."

He nodded. The stately Victorian was painted a cerulean blue that matched the waters of the bay behind it. The sun was setting over Willa Bay, staining the sky with shades of orange, pink, and purple that rivaled the tulips he'd seen earlier. He whistled. This place must have been something in its day.

"Would you mind if I took a quick look around outside? I'd love to check it out while there's still enough light to see." He'd developed an appreciation for old houses when he was a kid. His dad had changed duty stations every few years, but had always made sure to get an older house with character for his family, whether it be on post or in one of the surrounding communities. Jack Curtin claimed that living in a house with history was good for one's soul.

Zoe admired the sunset for a moment, then said, "Sure. I need to go inside to feed Celia's dog though. He's probably starving." She climbed up the stairs and inserted a key into the lock.

"I'll be there in a minute," he said.

She nodded and went inside, the door creaking behind her as it closed. He walked toward the corner of the house, circling a massive rhododendron bush covered in bright pink blooms. The grass was soft, almost soggy under his feet, and he wondered if it had rained earlier in the day. He rubbed his right knee, which hurt from the long plane ride and the change in climate between Charleston and Seattle. The chilly weather and frequent rain were two things about the Pacific Northwest that he hadn't missed in his travels around the world.

A wide porch wrapped prettily around the side of the house, but upon inspection, he could see that the railings were rotting in places. Even in the waning light, the peeling paint and cloudy windows were apparent. Celia hadn't been spending much time or money maintaining this place, not that he could blame her – it couldn't be cheap to own a house of this size.

Around back, he climbed up on the porch, testing it one foot at a time to make sure the boards wouldn't give under his weight. From here, the view of the sunset over the bay was breathtaking. He paused for a moment to take it all in. A soft breeze rustled the bushes nearby, carrying with it the aroma of the sea and reminding him a little of Charleston. He leaned against a post and stared out at the large island across the bay without really seeing it.

He'd dropped everything in Charleston to come to Willa Bay and he still didn't know who Celia was. Was she a long-lost relative like his father had asserted ages ago? Or was she a family friend? How did she have his phone number and address? If only his father was home so he could ask him.

He thought about contacting his sister, but he was fairly certain she knew less about Celia than he did, if anything at all. Besides, she was stationed in the Middle East, and he didn't want to bother her with this whole thing until he had more information to share.

A dog barked excitedly inside the house, and he reluctantly turned away from the view of the bay. If he and Zoe were going to discover anything tonight about his relationship with Celia, they should get started soon.

Zoe had left the door unlocked for him, so he didn't bother knocking before he entered the house. He stepped from the porch into a brightly lit entry hall. There appeared to be a living room off to the left, a staircase to the next floor just past that, and a closed door on his right. The house was chilly, but he didn't mind. He followed the laughter that echoed down the hallway from what he assumed was the kitchen.

"Shawn? Is that you?" Zoe's voice traveled down the hall. "I'm in here with Pebbles."

He dutifully followed her voice, finding himself in a large kitchen that hadn't been updated in several decades. Zoe was standing in front of a pot of coffee that had just started to percolate. In one corner of the room, a dog was noisily scarfing down a portion of kibble.

"I think Pebbles misses Celia," she said. "He was right

behind the door when I came in, and he hasn't left my side except to eat." As if on cue, the dog finished his food and trotted over to stand by Zoe.

Although he preferred larger dogs himself, he had to admit Pebbles was cute, with his rumpled fur and leathery black nose.

"Will he let me pet him?" Shawn asked.

She nodded. "He's really friendly." She leaned down to pet the dog. "Hey, buddy, this is Celia's friend, Shawn."

Shawn didn't know that "friend" was an accurate description for his relationship with Celia, but he didn't think the dog would care about semantics. Shawn walked over to Pebbles and knelt on the floor, running his hand over the dog's head. "Hi, Pebbles." The dog licked Shawn's face, leaving a trail of slobber across his nose.

Zoe covered her mouth, but couldn't hide the way the smile lit up her face. He liked the way the corners of her eyes crinkled as she tried not to laugh.

"What's so funny?" he asked, pressing his lips together to keep his face expressionless. "Haven't you ever been bathed by a dog?"

She broke out into laughter. "I've never really had a dog before, so I don't usually get that close. Is it normal for them to do that?"

He shrugged. "Sometimes. If they really like you." He rubbed Pebbles's head again and was rewarded by more slobber, this time across his fingers.

She wrinkled her nose. "I think I'll pass on the dog bath." She motioned to the coffee pot, which was now about half-full. "Do you want any? I know it's later in the evening, but I thought we might need a boost."

A woman after his own heart. "I never say no to a cup of coffee." He'd gone too many nights in the military without sleep and was no stranger to caffeine.

She poured coffee into a cup and handed it to him. "I think there's cream in the fridge, and I saw some sugar on the counter."

"No thanks. I drink it black."

She nodded approvingly as she poured herself a cup. "I do too. I guess growing up in the Northwest has made me a coffee snob, because I like to taste the coffee beans and not have their flavor obscured by anything else."

"I spent many years in Tacoma, but my love for plain coffee is more due to the lack of availability of cream or sugar in places I've been." He sipped the strong brew. "When I was overseas in the Army, it was just easier to drink it black."

She raised her eyebrows. "Ah. The military. That explains a lot."

He narrowed his eyes at her. "Explains what?"

"The short haircut and the fact that you live in Charleston but have a local phone number." She frowned. "I'm sorry I called you so late last night. I had no idea you were across the country."

"That's quite all right." He flashed her a smile. "I'm a night owl, and I'm glad you called then. If you'd waited until today, I probably wouldn't have been able to get a flight out to Seattle until tomorrow."

"Why did you come out here if you don't know Celia?" Her dark-blue eyes searched his face as she leaned against the counter.

"Curiosity, I suppose." He finished drinking his coffee and set the cup on the counter near the sink. "I've always wondered who she was, and I'd just finished up the house I was renovating in Charleston, so I was about to be out of a job and a place to live. It seemed like a good time to visit my dad too. He still lives in Tacoma."

Her eyes lit up. "He knows about Celia, right? Didn't you mention him talking to your mom about her?"

"I'm sure he knows, but he's off at his fishing cabin near Mount Rainier right now. The property is off-grid, and I'm not sure when he'll be back."

"Oh." She looked into her coffee cup, then back up at him. "So that's not going to help us at all."

He shook his head. "Nope. We'll have to figure it out some other way."

She finished her coffee, rinsed out both cups, and placed them in the dishwasher. "Okay. I think we should start with the desk in the living room. That's where I found your phone number."

"How did you know where to look?" he asked.

"Celia's oldest friend, Elizabeth, told me to find you in Celia's address book." She sighed. "But she already felt bad enough telling me that you existed. I don't think she'll divulge any more information about why you're the emergency contact."

"Geez. This is nuts." He ran his fingers through his hair as he stared at the floor. Now that he was out of the service, he'd let his hair grow a little longer, but the length still felt weird after so many years of biweekly buzz cuts.

"No kidding." She walked past him into the hallway with Pebbles trailing closely behind.

He followed her, but from this angle, the framed pictures on the hallway walls caught his eye. He pointed at a photo of a smiling couple in their early forties. "Is this Celia and her husband?"

She nodded. "Yes. I never met Charlie, but I heard he was a nice man. They didn't meet until she was in her late thirties, and they never had any kids." She peered at him. "Do you recognize either of them?"

He struggled to identify the happy couple, but couldn't

reconcile them with anything in his memories. "Sorry. No."

She sighed. "It was worth a shot."

He pointed at one of the group photos. "Is that you?"

She moved closer. "Yeah. That's Celia and me, with some of the others in our group. We're all involved in the wedding industry here, so we call ourselves the Wedding Crashers."

"Celia's still active in the community? That's impressive." His gaze moved over each one of the women in the picture. Out of the corner of his eye, he saw Zoe smile at the photo.

"She is. She was instrumental in making Willa Bay the wedding capital of the Pacific Northwest, and she's continued to support it ever since."

"I thought she owned the Inn." He studied the other photos on the wall.

"She does. But before our town became known for weddings, it was a resort community for city dwellers. When it became easier to travel out of the state, the industry declined. Celia didn't own the Inn at that point, but she lived and worked here. It was her idea to promote it as a wedding destination, and the idea caught on with the rest of the town."

The Inn must have been a beautiful location for a wedding. Although it was dark outside, he'd seen enough to know that the flowers, trees, grass, and view of the bay would be a perfect backdrop for a ceremony or reception.

"So, what happened to the Inn? Why did Celia close it down?"

Zoe straightened one of the picture frames. "Her husband died, and it just got to be too much for her to manage on her own. I'm sure she could have gotten someone to help, but I think she shut down a little when he passed away. It's been this way for as long as I've known her. Sad, though, huh?"

He nodded and moved down the hallway, away from the pictures. He ran his hand over the carved wooden balustrade of the staircase. Craftsmanship like that wasn't easy to find anymore. "This place deserves to be seen by people."

Zoe just smiled. "I'm curious to find out what's in her desk. I only looked through it briefly when I was searching for her address book." She walked over to the desk and pulled out the drawer. "There's nothing much in here." Disappointment etched her face.

Shawn picked up an address book from the top of the desk. "Is this where you found my phone number?"

She nodded and reached for it. "I'll show you." She flipped to a page near the back of the book and handed it to him.

His name and cell number were printed in scrawly blue lettering. "How did Celia get this?

"I don't know. Cell numbers aren't usually listed anywhere."

Shawn turned the page and found familiar names staring up at him. He stabbed his finger at the entry. "And my parents and sister are in here too." If only his dad were around to ask. It was killing him to not know why Celia had contact information for all of them.

"I think we should go through these next." Zoe held out a stack of photo albums and set them in the middle of the couch, taking a seat on an end cushion. She opened the first one, revealing recent images of herself and the other Wedding Crashers.

He sat at the other end of the couch. One by one, they scoured the albums, but the oldest began with Celia and Charlie's wedding around forty-five years ago. Other than Celia and Zoe, he didn't recognize anyone in the photos.

"It's no use." He leaned back against the couch. "It's getting late, and I haven't eaten all day. Do you want to go grab something to eat?" She hesitated, and he realized she might think he was asking her on a date. Normally, he wouldn't be opposed to that, but this wasn't the right place or time. "I mean, I don't have a car right now, so I'd appreciate the ride." He avoided looking at her directly.

She gathered up the albums in her arms and stood. "I haven't eaten much today either. Let me put these away, and we can head out."

Pebbles jumped onto the couch to take her place, and Shawn found himself petting the dog without even noticing.

"Shawn!" Zoe called out from the bookshelf. "Come see this!"

He eased away from Pebbles and crossed the room in three long strides. "Did you find something?"

"I don't know – maybe?" She'd opened a tin box that was about a foot square and a few inches deep and was scrutinizing a Polaroid picture so yellowed with age that she had to hold it a few inches from her face to make out the image. She handed it to him, blinking her eyes a few times as if to clear her vision. "It looks like a woman with a baby. There's some writing on the back. I see Celia's name. It's the only old photograph we've found – it has to mean something."

He took the photo from her. She was right about Celia's name, but he couldn't read the rest of the script on the back. He glanced at the ceiling and pointed at the desk. "The light's best over there." He carried the photo over to the desk.

"Oh! I think I remember seeing a magnifying glass in

here." She yanked the drawer open and pulled one out. He set the photo on the desk, and she held the magnifying glass over it.

"I think it says 'Anita, August fourteenth, 1960,'" Zoe said. "Does that mean anything to you?"

He grabbed for her hand to focus the magnifying glass, zeroing in on the baby's name. An icy chill shot through his body, from the tips of his hair to the soles of his feet. Her skin was soft and warm under his, and he realized he was still clutching her hand. He let go, muttering, "Sorry about that."

She scanned his face. "That's okay. You saw something though – what is it?"

He sighed. "That doesn't say Anita."

She gave him an odd look. "Okay?"

"It says Andrea. That was my mom's name, and that's the day after she was born."

He and Zoe stared at the photo. Why would there be a photo of his one-day-old mother with Celia? She must have been a close family member to have that privilege, so why had he only heard of her that once?

"If that's your mom ..."

"I know. I don't understand it either, but at least it definitely links Celia to my family." He stepped back from the desk and rubbed his weary eyes. It had already been a very long day. "I don't think we're going to figure this out on our own. With any luck, my dad will be back soon, and we can ask him. Let's go eat and then I'll figure out where I can stay in this huge house."

10

Cassie dropped the last egg white into the large bowl of the commercial-sized Kitchen Aid mixer and moved the lever until the beaters whirred briskly through the batter. It never failed to amaze her how so many different ingredients could come together in a bowl and quickly integrate into one delicious mixture. If only life could blend together so seamlessly. When the cake batter looked right, she turned off the mixer and removed the bowl, setting it on the table.

"What delicious treat are you making today?" Zoe asked from behind her.

Cassie jolted away from the counter, putting a hand over her heart. "You scared me! I didn't hear you come in."

"Sorry." Zoe shrugged and held up an empty mug. "I needed some coffee. I waved, but you didn't see me. You seemed to be entranced by whatever's in that bowl."

Cassie eyed the batter. "It's a lemon poppy-seed cake.

I'm testing it out for one of the smaller desserts for the Butler wedding this weekend."

Zoe sniffed the air. "Well, it smells great, and I know Angie Butler loves lemons. I think she mentioned it at least half a dozen times when we were deciding on the menu."

"I know." Cassie grinned. "I saw the triple underlined words in your notes." She moved the bowl closer to a row of mini Bundt cake pans and ladled a scoop of the batter into each of the indentations. "I'm going to drizzle a vanilla-lemon glaze on top once they're done."

Zoe nodded approvingly. "I'll be happy to test them later. At least I'll get something good out of this day."

Cassie scanned her friend's face. "Is Pearson that bad?"

Zoe sat down on a stool and leaned on the counter. "He's not great," she said in a low voice. "If he wasn't George's son-in-law, he never would have gotten the position." She sighed. "I know there's nothing I can do about it now, but this whole thing seems so unfair. I've worked for so long for that promotion, and he comes in here and steals it away from me." She pressed her lips together, then jumped down from the chair. "I can't let myself dwell on it, though, or I'll go crazy. I suppose it's really no different now than when Joan had the role. I still have my job, and that will have to do."

Cassie nodded. "How's Celia doing? Has anything changed?"

"Not really." Zoe frowned. "Shawn's at the hospital with her now."

Cassie raised her eyebrows. "He's still here?"

"I guess he's planning on staying until she wakes up." Zoe walked over to the coffee pot and filled her cup.

"Has he been able to reach his father? I'd be going crazy, wondering why Celia chose me as her emergency contact." Cassie brought the Bundt cake tins over to the oven and set them in, one by one.

"Nope, his dad's still out of town." Zoe carefully sipped her steaming coffee. "It's driving me crazy too."

Cassie sprayed the counter with disinfectant and wiped it down. "What is Shawn like? Have you spent much time with him?"

Zoe seated herself on the stool again. "He's nice – a little reserved. You can tell he's ex-military."

"Really? How so?" Cassie asked as she poured coffee into her own cup.

"I don't know. He looks like he works out, and his hair is cut shorter than I normally see around here."

Cassie grinned. "So, he's not bad to look at?"

Zoe's face turned pink. "That's not what I mean. He's not here for me to look at."

"Okay, okay. Is he staying at Celia's house?"

"Yep. He wasn't sure about it at first, but he seems to be settling in now. I think he planned to fix the back porch railing today."

"Aha. So he's handy too." Cassie winked at Zoe.

Zoe sighed and shot her a look of exasperation. "He's a carpenter, and he wanted to help out around the Inn."

Cassie watched her friend carefully. Zoe wasn't usually so easily flustered. Although Cassie had only been teasing her about Shawn, maybe there was something to it for Zoe to become so defensive.

A shadow appeared in the doorway, and Joan appeared. "Zoe? Can you please come to my office and help me show the booking system to Pearson?" She rolled her eyes. "After trying to teach him about the different wedding packages, my patience is about worn out."

Zoe took a deep breath. "Sure. I'll be right there." Joan

left, and Zoe drained the rest of her coffee and set it near the sink. "I'll see you later, okay?"

Cassie nodded. "I'm going to stop by the hospital to see Celia after Kyle gets off work today. I feel so bad I wasn't able to go yesterday."

"Don't worry about it," Zoe said breezily. "She's not awake right now anyway, and even if she was, she knows how busy you are with the kids and everything."

"I still feel bad." Cassie set her cup next to Zoe's and washed her hands. "Celia's done so much for me that it's the least I can do. Especially if she never wakes up." She swallowed against a lump forming in her throat. When Cassie had been going through her divorce, Celia had always been there to give her a pep talk or remind her that things would get better. Cassie didn't want to even entertain the possibility that Celia might never wake up.

Zoe crossed the room and gave her a quick hug. "She's going to be just fine. Okay, I've got to go teach Pearson how to not mess up our reservations. Wish me luck."

"Good luck," Cassie said to Zoe's back as she disappeared from sight. She hated seeing Zoe so depressed about her job situation. Her friend was generally a happy and positive person, but all of this must have thrown her for a giant loop.

It was almost time for Cassie to leave, but she wanted to make sure the front desk was stocked with fresh treats, so she got out the flour, sugar, eggs, and other ingredients to make a batch of peanut butter cookies. As she measured and mixed the ingredients by rote, then scooped the dough onto baking sheets, her mind drifted back to Zoe.

Life could change so quickly. Thank goodness Cassie's job was safe. Being the pastry chef for a small lodge may be a dead-end job, but between it and her cake-decorating side gig, she paid the bills. With the addition of the therapy sessions she was hoping to get Jace into, she needed every dollar.

"Cassie," a man said from the kitchen doorway as she took the cookies out of the oven.

She looked up and smiled at George. "Hey, I just finished baking some cookies. Do you want one?"

He didn't smile back at her. "Can you please come to my office when you're able to do so?"

Her stomach knotted immediately. After what he'd done to Zoe, she didn't know what to expect. "Sure. Let me get these out to the front desk and then I'll stop by to see you."

He nodded sharply, spun on his heels and disappeared back down the corridor.

Cassie removed the cookies from the cooling racks and filled a plate with them to take out to the lobby. The front desk was busy with check-ins when she got there, and a guest was just reaching for the last cookie on the plate. She smiled at everyone in line and swapped out the plates, beating a hasty retreat before she was run over by hungry guests. She placed the plate in the kitchen's dish sink and removed her apron.

Her steps plodded as she made her way to George's office. What was he going to say to her? She paused outside of his closed door for a moment, then took a deep breath and rapped on it.

"Come in," he called out.

She entered the room, and he motioned for her to take a seat.

"You're probably wondering why I called you in here today."

She nodded, but didn't say anything.

He looked at the photo of his family on his desk and

then back at her. "I'm really sorry, Cassie, but I can't let you use the Lodge's facilities anymore to bake and decorate the cakes for your side business."

She stared at him, her thoughts swirling around her brain like ingredients in a mixer, merging, but not forming a cohesive result. "Is there a problem I should know about?"

"No. It's just that, as you may know, my daughter, Lara, is home now, and she's starting her own cake business." He shifted in his seat, and an uncomfortable look crossed his face. "She – I mean, we – feel that it's a conflict of interest to let you work on your side business here."

"I see." Cassie knew she'd been lucky to use the Lodge's kitchens up until this point, but George's new ruling still stung. "I have cakes that need to be baked for this weekend and next. Can I use the kitchen until then?"

His gaze softened, and he gave her a tight smile. "Of course. I think it's fine for you to use it to complete this week's orders. I've always appreciated how hard you work at your job, and I hate to do this to you, but I've got to keep the peace at home. You understand, right?"

"I do." She paused. "Do you want me to continue as the pastry chef here?"

He leaned forward. "Definitely. We need you here."

Relief rushed over her. Finding a new baker's kitchen for her business wouldn't be easy, but at least she had a steady job. "Thank you."

"No, thank you." He smiled at her. "We've received nothing but compliments from guests about your baking. I'm sorry to have to change up our earlier agreement about the after-hours use of the kitchens."

"Don't worry about it." She stood from her chair. "I'll figure something out, and I truly appreciate you letting me use the kitchen in the past."

He nodded. "I'd better get back to work now, but I'm glad we had a chance to talk about this." He turned back to his computer, and she let herself out, closing the door behind her with a soft click.

Well, the other shoe had dropped. She had a job, but now what? Finding a place to bake wouldn't be easy, and she had orders lined up for at least the next six months. Her business was only a few years old – if she cancelled orders now, it wouldn't survive. She needed that money for bills and Jace's therapy.

She'd invested so much time and money into her side business. She groaned, thinking about all the hours she'd spent in cake decorating classes and practicing her skills afterward. That was all time she could have spent with her kids instead.

If her business failed, what would she do with all of the supplies she'd purchased over the years? She hadn't even paid back all of the money she owed on a small loan to cover her startup expenses. Despite trying to tell herself that she would come up with a solution, she couldn't help thinking that all of her hard work may have been in vain.

11

Meg

Meg artfully arranged a sprig of parsley around a chicken breast with blackening seasoning and used a pastry bag to dot the plate with little mounds of garlic mashed potatoes. She eyed the dish. Perfect. Every meal she plated was a chance to give a customer a work of art, even if they'd demolish it as soon as it was received. She slid it onto the warming shelf, where it was promptly picked up by Bailey, the waitress working that night.

Her phone rang from the deep pocket on the side of her jacket. She pulled it out and read the caller ID.

"Mom? Is everything okay?" she asked, trying to keep the fear out of her voice. It seemed like every time her mom called, she was sure it was going to be bad news.

Her mom ignored the question. "Hi, honey. Is this a good time?"

Meg looked around the kitchen. Dinner orders were stacking up, but this was her mom. "I can talk for a minute but then I've got to get back to work. What's up?"

"I won't take too much of your time. I was calling to invite you to a high tea at my house – with your sisters, of course. I thought it would be fun for all of us to get together." Her voice sounded far away, like she'd moved away from the phone.

"Is everything okay?" Meg asked again. Although her family was fairly close, her mother had never scheduled anything midday during the week before.

"Can't a mother have her children over once in a while?" Debbie sighed.

"Um. Doesn't Sam have to teach?"

"She's on spring break this week, so I thought it was the perfect time. You don't usually start work on Fridays until three o'clock, right?"

"Right." Meg fought to control the worry that was sweeping through her system. Why was her mom being so evasive? Had she heard bad news from her doctor?

"Oh, that's Libby on the other line. I'd better take this – I left her a message about the tea. Can I count you in?" Debbie asked.

"Of course." Meg would rather know now why her mother wanted to gather the family, but she'd have to find out the next day.

"Great. See you tomorrow at twelve thirty. Love you!" Debbie sang out before ending the call.

At least her mom's spirits were high. That had to be a good sign.

"Meg, are the other entrées for table ten ready?" Bailey called out from the kitchen entrance. "They've been waiting for their salmon for a while."

Meg slipped the phone back into her pocket and held up her hand in apology. "Sorry. I'll get them out to you ASAP. Just give me a minute."

Taylor heard the exchange and stepped away from the

grill with two salmon filets. The aroma of freshly grilled fish and dill hung in the air as he slipped them onto plates. Meg added the side dishes and handed them over to Bailey, who was hanging out at the end of the counter.

"Thanks!" Bailey placed the plates on a serving tray and left the kitchen to deliver the food.

"Is everything okay?" Taylor eyed her with concern.

"I think so. Sorry I got a little behind." She patted her phone pocket. "I don't usually answer my phone at work."

"Oh, I know. That's why I asked if everything was okay." His eyes searched her face. "Was it your mom?"

She nodded. "She wants to meet with me and my sisters tomorrow afternoon."

"Good news?" he asked. When she'd interviewed for the position at the Lodge, she'd told him she wanted to come back to town because her mom was ill, and he'd always made a point to ask her how Debbie was doing.

"I don't know." Her stomach twinged, and she made herself focus on the dinner orders. She'd found keeping her hands busy was the best thing to quell the anxiety.

He squeezed her shoulder, a comforting warmth radiating from his fingers. "I'm sure she's fine, but let me know if you need anything from me."

She gave him a half-smile. "Thanks, Taylor. I appreciate it."

"No problem." He shrugged and stepped back. "That's what friends are for." He quickly went back to the grill before she could respond.

She thought about what Cassie had said about Taylor having a crush on her. Meg still didn't think that was the case, but they had become good friends over the last year, and she was grateful to have him in her life.

The worry about her mother remained, overshadowing any thoughts about Taylor. Thankfully, the restaurant was slammed for a Thursday night, keeping her busy until closing. By the time she had everything cleaned and ready for the next day, she was too tired to think about anything but falling into bed and passing out.

The next morning, she took care of a few errands and then drove to her mom's house. Libby's car was already parked out front when Meg arrived, but Samantha wasn't there yet. Meg pulled her car in behind Libby's, turned the engine off, and stared at herself in the visor mirror. Dark crescents hung under her eyes, a testament to her lack of sleep last night.

She'd tossed and turned all night, worrying about why her mom had wanted to have her daughters over to her house. Although she'd attempted to conceal the evidence with a layer of foundation, Meg knew her mom would notice. She smiled at her reflection, hoping the forced cheer would become real.

Someone tapped on the passenger side window. Meg flipped the visor back up and opened the door.

Libby stood on the sidewalk, holding a large ring of keys. "Are you coming in?"

"Yeah. Sorry. I had something in my eye." Meg joined her on the sidewalk. "Did you just get here?"

Libby scoffed at her. "I've been here for thirty minutes already. I wanted to make sure Mom had someone to help her set things up." She gestured to her car. "I made some tea sandwiches, but I couldn't carry them all when I got here."

Meg raised an eyebrow. "Mom told me not to bring anything."

"Oh yeah, she told me that too, but I figured I should bring something anyway." Libby aimed her key fob at her car to open it.

Leave it to her older sister to show everyone else up.

"Do you need any help?" Meg asked, watching as Libby grabbed a short stack of covered trays off the floor of her minivan.

Libby flashed her a smile. "No, I'm good." Balancing the trays in one hand, she closed the minivan's door, then walked briskly up the sidewalk to the house they'd grown up in.

Meg followed behind her like a dutiful duckling. Her mom met them at the door, stepping aside to let Libby slip past her.

"Hey, Meggie." She gave Meg a hug.

Meg hugged her for longer than necessary, enjoying the comfort of being in her mother's arms. A tear slipped down her cheek, and she brushed it away before her mom could see it.

"Um, honey? Are you okay?" Her mom asked as she stepped back to look at Meg.

"I'm fine." Meg smiled at her. "Why?"

"Because you look like you haven't slept in a week, and your mascara is running."

"Oh, we were really busy last night. I was too amped up when I got home to get to sleep until late. And then I got something in my eye when I was driving." The little white lie she'd told Libby was coming in handy.

Her mother narrowed her eyes skeptically, but simply nodded. "I have everything set up in the dining room. Samantha called to say she'd be a few minutes late, but she'll be here soon."

She led Meg into the dining room, where Libby was busy setting up an impressive tray of tea sandwiches. "Libby made some extra sandwiches and cookies. I think she thought we were going to be feeding an army today."

Her mom's words were teasing, but she saw the loving glance she gave Libby. Meg winced. Although her mom had said not to bring anything, Libby never passed up a chance to show her younger sisters up.

A three-tiered cake stand next to the tray Libby was assembling held several different kinds of sandwiches, while another was piled high with scones and an assortment of petit fours. Juicy melon cut into cubes and tossed with purple grapes filled a large bowl. Smaller bowls held what Meg assumed was clotted cream and multiple jam varieties.

Meg sat down in front of the display of treats and breathed in the fragrant sweetness of the fruit, her stomach grumbling. "Wow. This looks delicious."

Her mother's chest puffed out. "Thank you. I had fun doing it. It's been a while since we took on a catering job with an afternoon tea theme, and I kind of missed it."

"You needed to take it easy," Libby said. "Working full-time in the business would have been too much for you while you were undergoing treatments and recovering afterward."

"Well, maybe now that she's done, she can take on more jobs." Meg watched her mother's face carefully.

"Maybe." Debbie smiled noncommittally at her. "Your sister should be here soon. I'm going to go fix the tea."

When she was out of sight, Meg whispered to Libby, "Has she said anything about the scan results?"

Libby shook her head as she sat down across from Meg. "Not yet. She refuses to tell me anything until Sam gets here."

The doorbell rang, and Meg heard her mom open the front door. "Do you think it's good news or bad?" Meg asked, her eyes flickering to the dining room entrance.

A shadow crossed Libby's face. "I don't know." She bit her lip and straightened a sandwich that had dared shift out of line on the second tier.

"Samantha's here," their mom called out from the front door.

Meg and Libby exchanged glances, and Meg steeled herself for whatever their mom wanted to tell them.

Samantha entered the kitchen, wearing a fuzzy, baby-blue sweater and denim jeans that hugged her petite figure. She smiled at her sisters before hanging her jacket over one of the high-backed wooden chairs. "I'm so hungry! Mom, you outdid yourself." She stood on her tiptoes and kissed her mom's cheek.

Debbie beamed. "Libby helped, but I had a lot of fun with it." She motioned for Samantha to sit down. "I'll grab the tea and we can start."

Debbie returned carrying a small pot of tea in each hand. When they were all seated around the table, she poured the tea into delicate china teacups with matching saucers. "You know, I've been collecting these teacups since I was a little girl, and they don't get nearly enough use. I think we should remedy that with a girls' tea party at least a few times a year."

"Sounds good to me." Samantha swallowed the last bite of a cucumber and cream cheese sandwich. "Next time, I'll make some sort of soup too. There's a recipe for a crab bisque I've been wanting to try."

"That would be lovely." Debbie sipped her tea, but Meg noticed she hadn't touched the scone and sandwich that she'd set on her plate.

"Mom." Meg's serious tone must have caught her sisters' attention because all conversation stopped. "I'm so glad to be here with all of you, but I think we're all wondering if you've heard from your doctor. It's been a week now."

Debbie nodded. "He called yesterday morning."

Meg held her breath.

A huge smile spread across their mom's face. "And I'm still cancer-free – at least for now."

"Mom, that's great news!" Meg jumped up from the table and enveloped her in a huge hug.

Samantha came around behind them. "I want in on this too," she said as she wrapped her arms around them both.

Libby watched them for a moment, then stood and set her hand on her mother's shoulder. There were tears in her eyes as she said, "Mom, I'm so happy for you."

The waterworks started for real then, with all four women crying tears of joy. Meg didn't usually consider herself to be terribly emotional, but right now, she was a wreck.

"Okay, okay." Debbie backed away and dried her tears with a napkin. "Now that we've got that out of the way, let's eat. Meg has to go in to work later, and I want to make sure we all have a chance to catch up. Everyone is always so busy I feel like I barely see you girls."

"We saw you last week at the Wedding Crashers get-together at Cassie's." Samantha's eyes twinkled. "I know you're getting old, but is your memory going too?"

Debbie slugged her youngest daughter lightly on the arm. "Haha, very funny. I remember. Sometimes, though, I like to spend time with just my girls."

"And we love spending time with you, Mom." Libby smiled at Debbie.

"Enough mushiness. Let's eat." Meg wiped her tears away with the back of her hand.

They all sat back down, and Meg filled her plate with sandwiches and cookies, suddenly starving. Knowing her mom was going to be okay was the best news she could ever ask for.

"Where's Kaya?" Meg asked Libby. "I was hoping to see

her today." Her four-year-old niece was adorable, with blonde curls, blue eyes, and chubby cheeks. Best of all, she thought her Auntie Meg was the coolest person on earth.

"She's with my neighbor, who has a little boy about the same age." Libby's gaze slid over to Debbie. "I wasn't sure if it was appropriate to bring her today."

Meg nodded. That made sense. If her mom had given them bad news, Libby would probably want to keep it from Kaya for a while because she was too little to understand.

Debbie wiped some powdered sugar from her mouth with a napkin and faced Samantha. "How's Brant doing?"

Samantha shifted in her seat and stared at the table for a moment. "He's fine. Just really busy with work."

"Any updates on the wedding?" Debbie asked. "Now that I'm feeling better, I'd love to help you plan it."

"No, not really any updates." Samantha reached for a scone and spread clotted cream across the top of it. "We still don't have a date set."

"I can help too," Libby said. "After all, I'm your maid of honor. Good thing you chose me because who knows if Meg will be around to help out." She eyed Meg with a look that wasn't entirely teasing.

Why was Libby acting like this? As far as she knew, she and her sister were on good terms. Had she missed something? "What do you mean?" Meg tried to keep her voice light and non-accusatory.

Libby sighed dramatically. "Only that you'll probably go back to Portland now that Mom is feeling better."

Debbie turned her head sharply, her eyes drilling into Meg. "Are you moving back to Portland?"

Meg glanced at Libby, then back at her mother. "I don't really know right now. I hadn't given it too much thought.

Maybe? If the right job comes up. There isn't a lot of room for career progression at the Lodge."

"Well, I don't want you to go, but I did like visiting you in Portland," Samantha said. "I think what I ate at the restaurant you worked at was the best meal I've ever had."

Meg gave her a faint smile. "Thanks. I appreciate that."

"You know, Mom, that gives me a good idea," Samantha said, mercifully steering the attention away from Meg. "We had fresh pasta with a basil cream sauce there that was astounding. Do you think we could work that into one of the catering menus?"

Debbie screwed up her face in thought. "I've been wanting to change out the ravioli menu with something more contemporary. That might just work." She, Samantha, and Libby dove into a discussion about the catering menus.

While the rest of them were talking about work stuff, Meg let her thoughts dwell on her own career. She didn't like the way Libby had insinuated that Meg wouldn't be there for her family, but her sister had been right. Now that their mom was officially on the mend, Meg could focus on the best move for her own future.

She liked working with Taylor at the Lodge and seeing her friends there every day, but she couldn't picture herself there long-term. Should she look into jobs back in Portland? Or a little closer, in Seattle? What would her life look like then? Her chest constricted at the thought of working for someone other than Taylor.

"Hey, Meg," Samantha said. "Did you hear what I asked?"

Meg shook her head to clear it. "No, I'm sorry. I was zoning out a little. What did you say?"

"I asked you if the Lodge might be willing to donate a night's stay to our school auction next month."

"I don't know. I can ask my boss." Meg took a swig of her tea, which was now cool.

"Thanks!" Samantha flashed her a smile. "Every little bit helps out the school. We're trying to raise money for a new playground."

"That's great. I'll make sure to ask him when I get to work." Meg checked her watch. "Speaking of which, I should probably head out. It's almost two thirty."

She said goodbye to her sisters, who stayed in the kitchen talking animatedly with each other while their mom walked Meg to the front door.

"You know I'm so proud of you, right, honey?" her mom said as they stepped out onto the porch.

Meg tilted her head to the side. "Proud of me?"

"Your dad and I love that you're doing what makes you happy, whether that's cooking in a restaurant halfway across the world or right here in Willa Bay. We miss you when you're away, but we just want what's best for you." Debbie hugged her. "This is your life to live."

Meg gazed out at the street. She'd tried to make an effort to see her parents a few times a year when she lived in Portland, but it hadn't always been easy. Living in Willa Bay for the past year had brought her closer to her mother than they'd ever been, even when Meg was still living in their home.

She wasn't sure how to respond to her mom's comment though because her own thoughts about moving were so conflicted. She finally settled on, "Thanks, Mom. I appreciate it. And don't worry. I'm not going to move halfway across the world." She hugged her mom again. "But I'd really better leave for work now."

"Love you." Her mom waved goodbye, not stopping until Meg was in the car.

Meg's stomach flip-flopped as she drove away from her

parents' house. They'd always encouraged all three of their girls to reach for their goals. Libby had married soon after college and settled into a house only a few blocks away from her childhood home, and Samantha had accepted a job at the local high school.

Meg was the only one who'd flown further away from the nest. It had been the right thing for her when she'd been fresh out of college, but was it where she saw herself now?

12

Zoe

The roar of a lawnmower's revving engine woke Zoe on Saturday morning. For a moment she lay in bed, confused. Living alone on the sprawling grounds of the old Inn, she wasn't used to hearing anyone else in the morning – but then she remembered that Shawn was staying at Celia's place. Zoe had seen Shawn briefly at the hospital a few times over the last three days, but they hadn't spent much time together.

She'd gotten the impression from him that he didn't think Celia could continue to live alone once she woke up, but Zoe didn't want to think about that possibility. The Inn was vitally important to Celia, and Zoe wasn't sure how long she'd survive in a long-term assisted living facility. But with Celia still in the hospital, it didn't seem like the right time to argue with him about it, so Zoe hadn't pressed the issue.

She fixed a hearty plate of pancakes, bacon, and eggs for breakfast, then dressed for work. With both an afternoon and an evening wedding scheduled at the Lodge, she'd be lucky if she got lunch or dinner. On the way out, she stopped in front of the old inn.

Shawn was working his way up the gentle slope leading to the gazebo. She waved to him, and the mower's engine cut off.

"Hey, Zoe." He wiped a handkerchief across his brow as he walked toward her, his gait uneven from what he'd told her was an old war injury. "I haven't had to cut this much grass since I mowed lawns for pocket money back in middle school. I don't seem to remember it being this exhausting, but maybe I was in better shape back then."

Her gaze slid involuntarily to the well-formed biceps peeking out of the short sleeves of the forest-green T-shirt he wore paired with faded blue jeans. How could he possibly have been in better shape? Heat rose up her neck and into her cheeks, and she twisted her head around to look back at the neatly cut lawn. Cassie would have a field day if she knew Zoe had been ogling Shawn's muscles.

She turned back to face him, hoping her blush had subsided. "Celia usually hires a landscaping company, but I think she forgot this year."

"I hope she doesn't mind. With all the rain you've received, the grass has been growing like crazy. I found the mower in the shed out back and thought I'd help out a little." He bent down to pick up a large rock embedded in the grass and threw it into a pile a few feet away. "Although all of the landscaping could use some TLC."

"The whole place could use some maintenance." Zoe eyed the fading paint on the inn's siding. "Celia isn't big on accepting help though."

He nodded. "I figured. From what you've said, she's one independent lady."

"Have you heard from your dad yet?" When she'd seen

him yesterday, he'd said his father might be home soon, and she was anxious for him to find out more about Celia.

"He called me back last night. I'm actually going down there in about an hour." He toed the ground. "Did you want to come with me?"

For a moment, she considered it because she so badly wanted to know the truth. She frowned. "I wish I could, but I'm heading into work, and I'll be staying late tonight."

He flashed her a grin, revealing a smile with two slightly crooked teeth. "Okay. I thought I'd ask since I know how badly you want to find out Celia's secret."

"Call me later tonight and let me know what your dad says." She looked up at the house. "How is Pebbles doing?" She'd intended to continue taking care of the dog while his owner was in the hospital, but Shawn had insisted on taking over the responsibility while he was living in Celia's house.

Shawn's face lit up. "He's doing great. I think he misses Celia, because he always sits on the floor near the couch, but he's been eating well, and he loves going for walks with me. We've been exploring the beach and some of the trails past your place."

"Oh, good."

"I grew up with dogs, and I've always wanted one of my own, but it seemed impractical when I was on active duty. I was away from home or out of town so often that I wouldn't have been able to spend much time with a dog." A wistful look came into his eyes. "I guess now that I'm officially retired, I can look into it."

She laughed. "It's weird to think of you being retired. You don't look that old."

"Hmm. And just how old do I look?" His eyes sparkled with mirth. "I haven't had anyone try to help me across the street yet."

She couldn't stop the giggle that bubbled up at the thought of Shawn needing anyone's help to cross a street. "I only meant that you seem young."

"I'm forty." His jaw clenched, and the humor left his eyes. "And I've seen way more than anyone should have at this point in their life."

He stared at the ground for a moment, and she sobered. Being in the military during times of war couldn't have been easy. Not for the first time, she wondered how he'd hurt his leg.

"Anyway." He trained his eyes on her and smiled to lighten the mood. "I should finish up here so I can drive down to see my dad."

She nodded. "Good luck." She returned to her car, climbing inside as the mower's engine roared back to life.

Good luck? She cringed. Why had she said that? Shawn's sudden retreat into himself had taken her by surprise. He'd seemed so easygoing whenever she'd seen him before, but although he'd attempted to hide it at first, there had been pain in his eyes when she'd commented on his age. He was definitely an interesting man, and she wouldn't mind getting to know him better.

Zoe drove the few miles to the Lodge at a slower speed than normal, hoping to put off seeing Pearson. She'd spent some time with him since he started, but he'd primarily been holed up with Joan as he learned her job. The more Zoe learned about him, though, the less she liked the man. Unfortunately, she didn't really have a choice if she wanted to keep her job.

When she arrived at the Lodge, Pearson was in the gardens conferring with Joan. He caught sight of Zoe, and made a point of checking his watch before shooting her a disapproving look.

Zoe's teeth pressed together so hard that her jaw hurt.

She didn't have a set schedule and would be at the Lodge for at least twelve hours that day. She didn't need her new boss acting like she was shirking her responsibilities. *Ugh.* Her "new boss." Bile burned her throat at the thought of working for Pearson when Joan left in a week.

Zoe pasted a bright smile on her face. "Good morning. I'm going to go over the checklist for the Damson wedding this afternoon. I'll be in my office if you need me."

"I wanted to review some of the event contracts with you today," Pearson said. "When will you have time for that?"

She mentally calculated her schedule. The Damson wedding started at noon and they'd be out by four. The next event didn't start until six, but she'd need to be on the ground by five-thirty at the latest.

"Does four-thirty work for you?" she asked.

He frowned. "I was hoping to do it earlier."

Joan stood behind Pearson her face hidden from his sight as she mouthed the words *I'm sorry* to Zoe.

Zoe briefly closed her eyes and nodded at Joan, then refocused her attention on Pearson. "I'm sorry, but with two big weddings today, I'm booked solid until then."

"If you'd gotten to work earlier, you'd have plenty of time to get everything done that's *required* for your job."

Zoe's jaw dropped, mercifully giving her teeth a break from the tension. She blinked at him. "Excuse me?" Had he seriously implied that the sixty-plus hours a week she spent at the Lodge weren't enough?

Joan touched Pearson's arm to get his attention. "We work a flexible schedule here because the events we manage don't always happen during the day."

He narrowed his eyes at Zoe. "That may have been true in the past, but an efficient workplace operates on a set schedule. Clients need to know that we're available for them during business hours. *I* need to know that you're here, doing your job. If one of us has to stay late for an event, that doesn't affect our set work hours."

Joan looked like she was going to say something, but she settled for shaking her head and sighing under her breath.

"Is this something George asked for?" Zoe asked. "He's always been happy with how we managed our time in the past." Pearson had only been there for a few days, and she already disliked him more than anyone she'd ever met.

Pearson's steely gaze made her insides boil. "I am in charge of event planning, and I think this will be a vast improvement on how things operated in the past."

Joan bristled noticeably, and Pearson gave her an oily smile. "No offense, of course. I'm sure you've done the best you could here."

Joan crossed her arms in front of her chest. "I'm going to grab a cup of coffee. Zoe, would you like to join me?"

"Sure. I've got to keep energized since I'll be here until late tonight." She wanted to give Pearson a piece of her mind, but Joan was giving her an out that could save her job.

Pearson sighed, as though Zoe were the laziest person alive. "Come find me when you have time to go over the contracts. I'd prefer sooner rather than later." He stalked away without giving them another look.

When they were alone, Zoe looked at Joan, her eyes wide. "Wow. He's a real piece of work."

Joan shook her head. "No kidding. Zoe, I'm so sorry to leave you with him. Maybe if I told George I'd stay he'd find something else for that jerk son-in-law of his to do."

Zoe's heart filled with warmth, and she gave her boss a big hug. "No, you've earned your retirement. Travel the world with your husband and kiss those grandbabies. I'll just have to figure out how to deal with Pearson on my own."

Joan's lips trembled. "I feel bad leaving you. I'd thought he'd be an idiot in a worst-case scenario, but he's shaping up to be a tyrant."

Zoe shrugged and said with forced cheer, "I'm sure I can win him over. Now, let's get that coffee."

They went to the kitchen together, purposefully going outside and accessing it through the exterior entrance to avoid any chance of seeing Pearson in the staff hallway. Cassie was in the kitchen, baking the rolls for the dinner crowd.

"What's wrong?" Cassie asked immediately upon seeing their faces.

"Pearson," Zoe and Joan said in unison.

Zoe laughed, a genuine smile spreading across her face. Now that she was safe in the kitchen with friends, she could momentarily forget her new boss's vitriol.

"That bad?" Cassie asked.

Zoe said in a whisper, "He's awful. He implied that I don't work hard enough at the Lodge because I got in at ten today."

Cassie's eyes widened. "You work harder than anyone I know." She went over to a side counter and came back with a plate full of cookies, offering it to Zoe and Joan.

"Thanks, Cassie. I'll have one in a minute." Joan walked over to the coffee pot and began filling two mugs.

Zoe shrugged. "He doesn't see it that way." She bit into a shortbread cookie, letting the buttery crumbs melt in her mouth. Tears formed in the corners of her eyes and she blinked them away. "But I have to get along with him. Joan and I have always worked closely together, and that's what's needed in this job."

"That should have been your job when Joan left."

Cassie selected a peanut butter cookie studded generously with chunks of chocolate.

"I agree." Joan came up behind them and slid a steaming mug of coffee in front of Zoe. "I should say something to George."

"It's too late. Pearson's already working here," Zoe said. "And nothing anyone says will change the fact that he's George's son-in-law."

"True." Joan grimaced. "But at least I'd feel like I tried to make the situation right."

"And I appreciate that." Zoe rested her hand on Joan's back. "You've been an amazing boss and mentor, and I've learned so much from you over the years. Remember when I was a fresh-out-of-college know-it-all?"

Joan laughed. "I remember. Maybe Pearson will grow into the job too."

Zoe scrunched up her nose and laughed. "I doubt it."

"So, you're just going to accept working for him?" Cassie asked, sipping her own coffee.

Zoe shrugged. "I don't have a choice right now, but maybe my future isn't at the Lodge." The thought was like a dagger to the chest. She'd invested so many years in the Willa Bay Lodge. What would it be like to start over somewhere new?

Her Pops wasn't getting any younger, and Luke had recently become engaged to his fiancée, Charlotte. With any luck, there would be nieces and nephews in a few years. In Willa Bay, she'd miss all of that. Her stomach clenched. Should she move back home to Haven Shores?

"You okay?" Joan asked.

Zoe set her coffee cup on the counter. "Yeah. Just thinking a little."

Joan patted her back. "Well, you deserve that." She finished her own coffee. "I'd better check in with Pearson.

He's been alone for ten minutes – who knows how many people he's alienated in that amount of time."

Zoe grinned. "Have fun."

Joan left, and Cassie peered at Zoe. "Are you really okay?"

Zoe's resolve to be strong evaporated, and a tear slipped from her eye. "I don't know."

Cassie led her into Taylor's office and closed the door. "Taylor won't mind if we borrow his office, and I think you could use the privacy."

Zoe sat down in one of the extra chairs across from Taylor's desk and angled it to face Cassie, who settled in the other one with her coffee. "I don't know what to do. I've been working here for a third of my life. I haven't seen my grandfather or my brother in way too long." She leaned forward and put her hands over her face, allowing the peaceful darkness to calm her thoughts. She sat back up and looked at Cassie. "I always thought this was where I'd be forever."

Cassie laughed. "I know the feeling. Ten years ago, Kyle and I were madly in love. Now look at us." Sadness filled her face for a moment, but then she eyed the door to the kitchen. "But change isn't always bad. Baking is something I've always loved, and now I get paid for it. If Kyle and I hadn't divorced, I'd probably be at home right now, bored out of my mind while the kids are in school." She looked straight at Zoe. "You'll figure out where you're meant to be too."

"I hope so." Zoe put her feet up on the seat of the chair and hugged her knees to her chest. "Because I can't see myself staying here and working for Pearson long-term."

"You're not the only one who's mad he and Lara moved back to town," Cassie said.

Zoe cocked her head to the side. "Why? What happened?"

Cassie sighed. "George informed me that Lara didn't like me using the Lodge's kitchen for the cakes I make on the side."

"Oh no. I can't believe he did that." Zoe dropped her feet to the floor. "What are you going to do?"

"I'm not sure." Cassie looked down at her hands and rubbed the back of her knuckles. "Commercial kitchens aren't easy to come by around here, and it would take forever to get the permits to bake out of my home – if I even had an oven that functioned consistently. George said I could use it for another week, but I've got orders for the next few months. I'm going to have to figure out something soon."

Zoe stared at her friend. She'd known Cassie even before her divorce, and she knew her friend counted on her cake decorating business to supplement what she earned at the Lodge. The gears in Zoe's mind turned, trying to come up with a solution. Solving someone else's problems was a welcome change from stewing about her own.

"Wait. I have an idea. Could you ask Debbie if you could use her catering kitchen?" Zoe's enthusiasm rose. "I don't think they accepted many jobs for the last two years, so the space may be available for you to use."

Cassie locked eyes with her, and Zoe could see the wheels turning in her head. "That's definitely an idea. I'll check with her when I get off work."

Zoe stood, feeling better than she had since she'd arrived at the Lodge that morning. "Speaking of work, I'd better get to it." She grimaced. "I wouldn't want Pearson to have any more ammunition to use against me."

They exited Taylor's office, and Zoe walked over to the

door that led to the staff hallway. "Thanks for the talk, Cass."

Cassie smiled brightly at her. "Of course. And I should be the one thanking you. I can't believe I didn't think about Debbie's kitchen before."

"Glad to be of service." Zoe waved at her and pushed the door open, silently wishing that the hallway would be empty. It was, although she could hear Pearson talking with Joan in her office a few doors down. Zoe scurried into her own office and shut the door.

She tried to focus on her work, but she could still hear Pearson, and his voice intruded on every thought she had. She pushed her chair back and stretched her legs, surveying her office. She'd always loved working at the Lodge, but maybe it was time for a fresh start somewhere else.

13

Shawn

Shawn left Willa Bay about two hours after Zoe stopped by. Tacoma, the city where his father lived, was about a three-hour drive from Celia's house. He couldn't believe how much the Seattle metropolitan area had grown in the years that he'd been away in the Army. In the late morning, the traffic on Interstate 5 was manageable, but he wasn't looking forward to the drive home in rush hour traffic.

He'd finished mowing the lawn, but he'd have to edge the flower beds another time. It seemed like everywhere he turned, there was something else to do at the Inn. It gave him something to do, though, as he waited for Celia to wake up. He wouldn't let himself think of the possibility that she might not come out of her coma.

Unlike Zoe, he wasn't under any misconception that Celia would be able to live alone at the Inn when she was released from the hospital. With the condition of her home, it just wasn't safe for her. He wasn't sure how he was going to convince Zoe of that though.

The traffic slowed to a crawl as he neared Seattle. The Space Needle rose above the city with Lake Union sprawling at its feet. Sun glinted off the metal siding of the watercraft floating on the lake, including houseboats, pleasure boats, and commercial vessels. The air quality in this part of the freeway was diminished, with car engines spilling fumes into the narrow, almost tunnel-like passage through the skyscrapers of downtown.

When the traffic broke free, he was well south of Seattle and closing in on Tacoma. His father lived in an older part of the city, close to Point Defiance Park, in a neighborhood composed primarily of Craftsman-style homes from the early 1900s. The tree-lined lanes hadn't changed much since he'd lived there as a teenager, although he approved of the newish ordinance that eliminated parking on one side. As a freshly licensed driver in his mom's new car, he'd accidentally sideswiped a vehicle parked along the crowded street. He'd spent way too many hours working off that debt.

Finally, having parallel parked in front of his dad's house, he got out of the car and stood on the grass median for a minute, stretching out the kinks in his arms and legs from the long drive. Jack Curtin's cheery yellow house was two stories tall, with a half story above it in the attic – Shawn's old room. Well-groomed flowering shrubs surrounded the porch. From the scent of freshly cut grass permeating the air, it appeared his dad had spent some time with the lawnmower this morning, just as Shawn had.

Shawn climbed the four stairs to the front porch and rang the doorbell, feeling like a stranger in front of the home where he'd lived for many years. Heavy footsteps plodded along the hardwood floors in the entry hall, and the door swung open.

"Shawn!" His dad pulled Shawn against his chest, hugging him tightly. "It's been too long. How've you been?"

Shawn smiled. It was good to be home. He'd moved so much that he'd never gotten too attached to any location, and while he'd loved Charleston, it wasn't his home yet either. Home was where his loved ones were.

Shawn stepped back to assess his father. "I've been good, Dad. How about you?"

"I've been good too. My knee has been bothering me, but what else is new?" He chuckled and led Shawn into the living room next to the door. "The doc says I'll probably have to get it replaced soon."

Jack wobbled a little as he made his way to the easy chair he'd had for as long as Shawn could remember, one Shawn's mom had reupholstered several times. Although everything inside and outside of the house was neat and tidy, the living room looked exactly the same as it had when Shawn had lived there years ago. His father was getting older, and although Shawn had tried to talk him into moving to a smaller place that would need less maintenance and wouldn't be so full of memories of his mom, Jack had refused.

His dad leaned back in the chair and kicked up the footrest. "What brings you to Seattle? Did you finish up the house you were working on in Charleston?"

Shawn nodded as he sat down on the couch across from his dad. "I did. The sale should close sometime next week." He wasn't sure how to ask about Celia, so he stuck with small talk. "How was your fishing trip?"

His dad brightened. "Good. I caught four trout up at the lake one day, and six another day." He laughed. "I've got so much fish in the freezer now I don't know what to do with it all. Hey, do you want some?"

Shawn grinned. "Maybe." He looked at the picture of his mom on the side table closest to his dad. It was taken when she was in her early fifties, about a year before she died. She was lovely, with wavy brown hair to her shoulders and piercing blue eyes. He'd often been told he looked like her. He got up to take a closer look at the picture, searching for any resemblance to Celia.

Shawn knew his dad was watching him closely, sensing something on his son's mind. "So, I ask again, what brings you to Seattle? You seem troubled."

Shawn sat back down on the couch and faced his father. "Things are fine with me. I had a little time off and was looking for the next thing to move on to." The tension in his shoulders was mounting with every minute he put off asking his dad about Celia. He leaned forward. "But that's not why I'm here."

His dad straightened as though he recognized the seriousness in his son's voice. "What is it?"

"Do you remember that time I heard you and Mom arguing about someone named Celia? I must have been about nine or so." He focused on his dad's face. Would Jack tell him the truth about Celia, or had that secret died with his mother?

Jack's face was expressionless. "I remember. You were quite young then." He peered at Shawn. "But what brings this up?"

Shawn took a deep breath. "Celia James is in the hospital. Her neighbor found my name listed as her emergency contact."

Jack focused on his hands, folded in his lap. "Celia James. I haven't thought of her in a long time." He looked up at Shawn. "Your mom didn't want you to know about her, but I think it's important that you do."

Shawn's heart beat faster, and he scooted to the edge of the sofa. After all these years, he was finally going to find out about Celia. "Who is she?"

His dad sighed and shifted in his seat. "Celia is your grandmother."

Shawn blinked a few times, trying to process everything. "What do you mean she's my grandmother? I knew both Grandma Betty and Memaw."

"Grandma Betty was Celia's cousin. I don't know the whole story because your mom wanted nothing to do with Celia, but from what I understood, Celia got pregnant and decided to let Betty and her husband adopt your mother. They hadn't been able to have children and were eager to become parents." Jack fixed his eyes on Shawn, as if trying to gauge his son's reaction. "I know, it's a lot to take in."

Shawn sat back. "So, Grandma Betty and Grandpa Delbert weren't really my grandparents?"

His dad shrugged. "They were the only parents your mother ever knew, and the only ones that mattered to her. Your mother didn't want Celia in her life, even after she'd grown up and Celia tried to reconnect with her."

"Wow." Shawn had expected that Celia might be a distant relative, but he never would have expected the truth. "So, she wanted to reunite with Mom, but Mom wouldn't let that happen?"

He'd never thought of his gentle mother as a cruel person, so she must have had a good reason to do what she did. An image of Celia looking small and lonely in her hospital bed passed through his mind. Zoe cared a great deal about Celia, so she couldn't be that bad.

His father pursed his lips, then sighed and said, "Your mother was a wonderful woman, but she had a stubborn streak a mile long. She'd made up her mind that Celia didn't care about her and had given her up without a thought – and that was that. She never found it in herself to forgive Celia."

"But that wasn't true, right?" Shawn asked. "If Celia couldn't care for the baby, wasn't it better to give her up?" It was odd to think of his mother as a little baby, abandoned by her birth mother.

Jack's face was troubled. "I tried to make her see that, but she wouldn't change her mind. After that argument you witnessed, we never spoke of Celia again. If Celia contacted your mom after that, I never knew about it."

"But why would Celia have listed me as her emergency contact?" Shawn asked. "And how did she have my cell phone number?"

"I don't know. Back then, Celia so badly wanted to reunite with your mother. Maybe she hoped to eventually have a relationship with you too. I'm sure there are ways to get contact information for anyone nowadays." His dad's eyebrows lifted slightly. "I take it she's not doing well, or she'd have told you all of this herself."

"She fell in her house and hit her head last week. She hasn't regained consciousness since then." Shawn sighed. "I can't believe I have a grandmother I never knew."

"Well, I hope you have a chance to get to know Celia. I still think your mom was overly stubborn about her. Maybe you'll be able to make things right." He pushed the footrest in and rocked the chair up to stand. "I'm going to fix some lunch. Do you want any?"

"Sure." Shawn wanted to know more, but it didn't sound like his father knew anything else. They walked into the kitchen where Jack gathered two cans of tuna from an upper cabinet, and some mayo and pickles from the fridge.

133

"Extra pickles, right?" His dad asked as he prepared the tuna salad.

Shawn grinned. "You remembered." The family joke had always been that a jar of pickles didn't last long with Shawn in the house.

"How could I forget? Your mom always made me run to the store for pickles when she was making tuna salad sandwiches because hers had mysteriously disappeared." His dad smiled at the memory.

"I miss her." A vision of his mom flashed into his head, filling him with warmth. She may have teased him about his infatuation with pickles, but she'd always tried to have her family's favorite foods on hand. It was one of the many ways she demonstrated how much she loved them. He took the plate his dad handed him, bit into the sandwich, and grinned. "Tastes just like how Mom used to make it."

"That's because I used her secret ingredient." His dad held his hand up to the side of his mouth and whispered, "Some pickle juice mixed in with the mayo. Shh. Don't tell anyone." He passed Shawn a bag of potato chips and took a huge bite of his own sandwich.

"That explains why I like her recipe so much." Shawn took a swig of water from the glass his dad set in front of him.

"Anything else new with you?" His dad asked in between bites. "Are you seeing anyone?"

Shawn thought about the way Zoe had broken out into laughter when Pebbles had licked his nose, and his pulse quickened. There was something about Zoe that caught his attention every time he saw her – the way she took charge of a situation and the fierce loyalty she showed toward Celia. When she'd seen him mowing the lawn that morning, he'd almost thought there had been something between them, but she'd never given him any indication of romantic interest. It was probably for the best though – she was the type of woman to settle down with, and he wasn't sure where he'd be next month, let alone in a year.

"Nope. Not seeing anyone." Shawn reached into the chip bag to grab a few. "You?"

His dad laughed. "Son, your mom was the love of my life. It'd take a heck of a woman to even come close to her."

"So, we're both going to be bachelors for the rest of our lives, huh?" Shawn said.

His dad shook his head. "I think the right woman for you will come along soon. There's hope for you yet." He flashed a smile at Shawn before finishing off his sandwich.

Maybe she already has. At that thought, Shawn stood abruptly and carried his empty plate over to the sink.

"Do you have any pictures of the house you remodeled?" His dad asked as he joined Shawn at the sink. "I'd love to see it."

Grateful for the subject change, Shawn placed their rinsed plates in the dishwasher and looked up at his dad. "I took hundreds of photos of it. You're going to love the history in this house."

They sat together on the couch with Shawn's phone, swiping through the before and after images of the house in Charleston.

"You do good work." Jack admired the renovated kitchen. "I like how you kept some of the period details but updated it for modern-day living."

His father's praise meant a lot to him. "Thanks, Dad."

An image of the Inn at Willa Bay flashed into his mind. What he would give to have the money to renovate that place. With proper care, he knew he could restore it to its former glory. That was only a dream though. Even if Celia eventually sold it, he couldn't afford the annual property taxes on it, let alone the purchase price or cost of a full-scale remodel.

"Tell me about the house's history," his dad said, interrupting Shawn's musings. "I bet this home has a story to tell." He handed the phone back to Shawn.

"That it does." Shawn had researched the Charleston property while he'd been living in it, and he launched into a long summary of what he'd discovered.

The two of them hung out until after dinner, at which point Shawn said he needed to get back to Willa Bay. His father extracted a promise from Shawn to come see him before he returned to Charleston.

"I will, Dad. I love you." Shawn hugged his father tightly. Seeing Celia in the hospital had made him realize how quickly things could change, and he didn't want to leave anything left unsaid.

"I love you too." His father returned the hug, then clapped him on the back. "Take care, son, and don't be afraid to let your guard down once in a while. You never know what you might find."

"Thanks, Dad." Shawn walked down the sidewalk to his car, waving as he pulled away from the curb. He had mixed feelings about returning to Willa Bay. Although he now knew Celia was his grandmother, would he ever have a chance to get to know her? Whatever the case, it was nice to finally have the truth out in the open. He couldn't wait until he was back at the Inn and could see Zoe in person to tell her what he'd found out.

When he arrived in Willa Bay, Zoe was still at work, so he busied himself with some small repairs at the Inn. As soon as he saw her car in the driveway, he walked over to her cottage to tell her his news.

"Hey." She looked up at him in surprise as she got out of her car. "I was planning on coming over to see what you'd found out."

"I couldn't wait to tell you." He let the suspense build until Zoe raised an eyebrow at him. "Celia is my grandmother."

She shut the car door and stared at him. "Are you serious?"

He nodded. "She gave my mom up for adoption right after birth. The woman I knew as my grandmother was actually Celia's cousin."

"Wow." Zoe blinked several times. "I definitely wasn't expecting that."

"Me neither." Shawn was quiet for a moment. "I can't believe my mom never told my sister or me about Celia."

"She must have had her reasons," Zoe said.

"I guess, but I can't imagine what they could have been. That's a big secret to keep." Shawn stuffed his hands in his pockets. If Celia hadn't been hurt, he may never have learned about her existence.

"Yeah. I really hope Celia wakes up soon so she can tell us what happened." Zoe gestured to her cottage. "I was just about to make a late dinner. Did you want to join me?"

"Sure. I'd like that." He gave her a wide smile, then followed her inside her home. So far, Willa Bay hadn't been what he'd expected, but between Zoe and the mystery surrounding his biological grandmother, he was looking forward to staying awhile.

14

Cassie slid a tall wedding cake off the wooden board on the floor of her minivan and onto the small wheeled cart she used for transporting larger cakes. The wedding ceremony was taking place in a local Presbyterian church, but they were hosting a big reception at the nearby Elks hall situated along the Willomish River. She rolled the cart through a back door and into the main room, which had already been decorated in the wedding colors: silver and navy blue.

She'd delivered cakes and attended events here in the past and knew the layout well. There was a benefit to living in the town where you'd grown up. She approached the entrance to the kitchen at the back of the room. If the racket and delicious aromas coming from behind the closed door were any indication, the catering staff would be taking care of any last-minute preparations before dinner was served at six thirty.

The wedding party wasn't due to arrive for another

hour, and Cassie didn't see anyone who appeared to be in charge, so she ducked into the kitchen for a minute. "Hey," she said.

Four people were hard at work prepping food. One was sprinkling herbs on the top of a massive dish of mashed potatoes, while two others were mixing up something in vats that looked like salad dressing. A woman looked up from loading plates and silverware onto a cart that was twice as big as Cassie's and broke into a smile. "Cassie! I heard you were doing the cake tonight. I hoped I'd get to see you."

"Hey, Gabby. It's been a while." Cassie gave her a hug. Gabby Tyrane was an old friend of hers from high school and had started her own catering company a few years ago. "It's good to see you." She sniffed the air. "Something smells great."

Gabby nodded to a row of chafing dishes on the far counter. "It's the beef medallions. They're always a big hit at wedding receptions."

"I kind of wish I was staying for dinner," Cassie joked.

"Stop by later tonight and I can slip one into a box for you." Gabby winked at her. "How'd the cake turn out?" She lowered her voice so her employees milling around the kitchen couldn't hear her. "This bride is super fussy, so don't be surprised if she nitpicks."

"There's not much I can do about it at this point if she doesn't like it, but I think it turned out well," Cassie said. "Do you want to see it?"

Gabby surveyed the kitchen. Seemingly satisfied with everyone's progress, she nodded. "Of course."

Cassie led her out to the cake, which was still on the cart. "Actually, I wasn't sure where they wanted me to put it, and I couldn't find the wedding coordinator."

Gabby laughed. "Oh, she had to leave to take care of

an errand for the bride. She should be back any minute." Gabby took a closer look at the cake and sucked in her breath. "It's gorgeous. Cassie, you've outdone yourself on this one."

"You don't think she'll find anything to complain about?" The cake was composed of four square tiers, placed offset from each other. She'd decorated the white fondant with navy-blue flowers and silver fleur-de-lis accents. In her opinion, it was one of the best she'd ever done, and she'd made sure to take several photos of it for her portfolio.

"Uh, I don't see how she could." Gabby walked around the cart. "I love the flowers. They're so detailed and cute."

"Thank you." Cassie glowed at her friend's praise. Hearing people compliment her creations increased her confidence and certainty that this career was worth the effort and expense she'd invested in it. "I hope the bride feels the same. She had very definite ideas of what she wanted it to look like."

The back door cracked open, and they both looked to see who'd come in.

"That's the wedding coordinator. I'd better get back to work. It was nice seeing you again," Gabby said. "We'll have to get together sometime outside of work."

"That'd be great." Cassie smiled at Gabby, who tossed a little wave at her and the person who'd just entered before scurrying back to the kitchen. Cassie didn't recognize the harried woman striding toward her. "Hello," Cassie said to her.

"Hi, I'm Tia, the wedding coordinator. I'm so sorry I wasn't here when you arrived." She brushed aside a wisp of hair that had escaped her tight bun and checked the small tablet she held in her hands. "You must be Cassie?"

"I am." Cassie nodded at the cart. "I wasn't sure where to put the cake."

Tia tapped on the tablet screen, then looked back up at Cassie. "They want it over in the corner opposite the buffet tables." She gestured to a round table, about four feet in diameter, near the wide windows overlooking the river. "Do you need any help?"

"I'll need some assistance getting the cake onto the table." Cassie rolled the cart over to the table, which was clad in a navy-blue linen that matched the flowers on the cake.

Together, they moved the cake into place and rotated it until the ceramic bride and groom on top were facing into the room.

"It's beautiful. I think they're going to love it." Tia rummaged in the messenger bag strung over her shoulder and pulled out an envelope marked "Cassie." She held it out and Cassie took it.

"Thanks." Cassie refrained from checking the envelope until she could do so privately. She'd found it best not to spoil the wedding mood with talk of money, and if the clients had stiffed her on the payment, she would figure that out later.

"You're welcome." Tia scanned the room. "Everything is coming together so nicely." Her voice was filled with relief.

Cassie raised an eyebrow. "Did something not go well earlier?"

Tia blushed. "It's only the first wedding I've done on my own. I just set up shop in Willa Bay a few months ago."

That explained why Cassie hadn't met her before. "Well then, welcome to Willa Bay. If you ever need anything, let me know. You have my phone number."

"Thank you." Tia sighed. "Everyone's been so nice

here. I thought it would be more cutthroat with so many service providers."

Cassie laughed. "Nope. Not usually. There are plenty of weddings to go around. The whole industry benefits when clients and guests are happy and spread the word about the amazing weddings in Willa Bay."

"Hmm. I never thought about it like that before." Tia eyed her watch. "I'd better get going though. I still have a few more things to check on before everyone arrives."

"Good luck." Cassie snapped a few photos of her masterpiece against the backdrop of the wedding decorations, then grabbed the cart handle and exited the building.

As she lifted the cart into the van, she thought about what she'd told Tia. Usually, service providers in Willa Bay were more than happy to support one another. Lara Camden was the exception. Cassie's mood darkened as she got behind the wheel and drove out of the parking lot.

She still hadn't had a chance to talk to Debbie Briggs about using her catering kitchen, but that needed to be a top priority. She had until next weekend to find a new place to bake her cakes, which didn't leave much time if Debbie's didn't work out.

She'd planned to meet Zoe and Meg for the late-night happy hour at their favorite cafe after Zoe got off work, but Cassie wanted to stop at the hospital and check on Celia first. It had been a few days since she'd last visited.

When she got to Celia's hospital room, a tall man with brown hair was sitting in an armchair by Celia's bedside. He stood when she walked in.

She paused in the doorway. Was this Shawn? She'd never met him, but he fit Zoe's description: tall, fit, and sporting a short haircut.

"Hi." She walked closer and held out her hand. "I'm Cassie, a friend of Celia's."

Recognition dawned on his face as he reached out to shake her hand. "Oh, Zoe's mentioned you. I'm Shawn Curtin. Nice to meet you." He looked over at Celia. "I can leave if you want some time alone with her."

Cassie waved him off. "No, no. That's fine. I wasn't planning on staying long. I just like to check on Celia and let her know that we're all here and pulling for her to get better." She reached for Celia's left hand and covered it with her own as she sat next to her in a plastic folding chair.

The elderly woman didn't look much different from the last time Cassie had seen her. Her face was pale, but her breath was steady, and it looked like the hospital staff had recently washed the cloud of white hair that spread out across the pillow.

"Have the doctors given you any idea of what to expect?" Cassie asked.

He shrugged, then stretched out his arms and back, as though he'd been sitting for a long time. "Not really. They've been pretty vague. She's still healing from her hip and leg surgery. Once she's recovered enough, even if she's not awake, they'll move her to a rehabilitation facility where they'll be able to exercise her muscles while she's in bed."

"Oh." Cassie stared at Celia. She had rarely seen her elderly friend sit still for very long, so it was hard to see the once-lively woman this motionless. "I wonder if she knows what's going on."

"I like to think so." Shawn sat back down across from Cassie. His gaze was soft as he looked at Celia and squeezed her hand. "Sometimes she seems to react to what I say."

Cassie remembered Zoe mentioning that Shawn planned to visit his father the day before. "Did you have a chance to see your father yesterday?"

"I did." The overhead vents blew a strand of Celia's hair into her eyes, and Shawn moved it to the side with surprising tenderness. He was different than she'd expected from a career-military man.

"What did he say about Celia?" Cassie looked directly into his eyes.

He sighed and looked down at Celia. "He said she's my mother's birth mother."

"Celia's your grandmother?" Cassie focused on Celia's face. She could have sworn that her lips had started to curve into a smile, but then any expression faded from her face. "I thought she and her husband didn't have any children."

He peered at Celia as though he'd also seen the faint glimmer of a smile. "She gave my mother to a cousin of hers to raise."

"Oh." Cassie wasn't sure what else to say. "So, your mother never knew about Celia?"

He frowned. "No. She knew. She just didn't want Celia to be a part of her life."

"But you feel differently?" Cassie asked. She suspected she already knew the answer based on how he treated Celia.

He sighed and ran a hand over his short, bristly hair. "I want a chance to get to know her and find out why she did what she did." His eyes were bright with tears as he looked at Celia. "I only hope I get that chance."

A sense of sureness ran through Cassie, although she didn't know where it came from. Her life was falling apart, but for some reason, she knew things would be okay with Celia. "You will."

They sat together for another half hour, chatting about a random assortment of topics until Cassie had to leave to meet her friends. She also wanted to call Debbie as soon as she had a chance.

"I'm supposed to meet Zoe and another friend of ours, Meg, at a local cafe. Did you want to come?"

He hesitated for a moment, then smiled. "Nope, I think I'm going to stay here with Celia for another hour. It's too dark to get much done around the Inn right now, so I might as well stay and keep her company. I hope you have a good time with everyone." He added hesitantly, a faint blush tinting his cheeks, "Tell Zoe I said hi."

Cassie grinned. She'd thought there was something going on between him and her friend. "I will. Goodnight." She gathered her belongings and left the hospital room.

Cassie waited until she was out of the hospital and in her car to call Debbie. The air outside was brisk. While she'd been visiting with Shawn and Celia, the sun had set, causing the temperature to drop. A blast of wind hit her, and she shivered as she hurriedly got into her car and turned on the engine to warm it up.

With the heat turned on full blast, Cassie dialed Debbie. The phone rang twice, then Debbie answered. "Hello?"

"Hi, Debbie, it's Cassie."

"Oh hi, Cassie. How are you doing?" Debbie's warm voice on the other end of the phone lifted Cassie's spirits. Cassie had been friends with Debbie's daughters since she was a small child, so talking to her was almost like talking to her own mom.

"Pretty good. But I do have a favor to ask of you."

"Sure. What is it?" Debbie asked.

Cassie took a deep breath. "I was hoping to borrow your catering kitchen for a few weeks, maybe more. I need somewhere to bake and decorate the cakes for my side business."

"Oh." Debbie was quiet for a moment. "Hmm ..."

Cassie's heart sank. This wasn't going to work out. "If you can't do it, though, don't worry about it. I can find somewhere else."

"No, no, honey. I'm sure we can work something out. It's just that since I'm feeling better now, Libby and I were planning to bid on more catering jobs. We'd like to get the business back up and running full time." A TV blared in the background on Debbie's end of the line and Cassie heard her say, "Peter, can you turn that down please? I'm on the phone." The noise lessened and Debbie came back on to the call. "What happened with baking cakes at the Lodge though?"

Anger welled up in Cassie's chest, and she fought to swallow it down. "Lara Camden. She told her dad that she doesn't want me using the Lodge kitchen for my side job."

"Because she's now a competitor of yours." Debbie sighed. "What a spoiled little brat. I never did like that girl."

Cassie grinned. "Me neither. Unfortunately, I've only got about another week to use the Lodge kitchen and then I need to move my business to another location."

"Okay. We'll make this work, at least until a better solution presents itself. I know you've put a lot of effort into your cake decorating business and I'd hate to see you lose that. How about you give Libby a call early next week, and she can put you on the schedule to use our catering kitchen."

Cassie thought her heart might burst with gratitude. "Thank you! Thank you so much!" Happy tears blurred her vision. "I promise I'll locate to another space as soon as I can. George didn't give me much notice that I needed to move, and I didn't know what I was going to do."

"Don't worry," Debbie said. "Everything will work out. Now, I'd better get back to watching *Wheel of Fortune* with Peter. He always ends up with more money than me anyway."

Cassie laughed. "Good luck. And thank you again. You have no idea how much this means to me."

"No problem. Good night." Debbie hung up the phone.

Cassie leaned back against the seat of her car and closed her eyes for a moment. Crisis averted, at least temporarily. Having permission to use Debbie's catering kitchen was a welcome reprieve that gave Cassie some breathing room. If she was lucky, maybe everything else in her life would fall into place just as easily.

15

Meg

After helping Taylor and the rest of the kitchen staff clean-up for the night, Meg left the Lodge to join her friends at their favorite place to eat, Pondera Bistro. As she walked to her car, she checked her phone's voicemail. It had vibrated an hour or so ago, but she'd been too busy putting food back into the walk-in refrigerator to answer it. Now, she pressed play to find out what the caller wanted.

"Hi, Meg," a familiar voice said, "it's Tammi Gables. How are you doing? Have you given any thought to moving back to Portland? I'm calling because I heard through the grapevine about a sous-chef position at La Lobessa, and I think you'd be perfect for it. The chef's a friend of mine, so I bet I could snag you an interview. Let me know what you think. I'd love to see you again. Talk to you soon."

Meg stuffed the phone back in the pocket of her wool coat and pulled the heavy fabric tighter against her body.

She walked quickly down Willa Bay Drive as she considered Tammi's voicemail. With her mom getting a clean bill of health, Meg was free to return to Portland and resume her old life. But was that what she wanted?

She moved on autopilot toward Pondera Bistro, lost in thought. There were so many things to consider. Even if she got the job, she'd have to rent an apartment in Portland and move everything from her place in Willa Bay. But she liked her life here. Portland had been wonderful career-wise, but her demanding job hadn't left her any time to develop strong friendships like the ones she'd made in Willa Bay.

Pondera Bistro was located on the river side of Main Street. On nice summer days, Meg loved to eat on their back deck overlooking the water. Today, though, it was too cold to eat outside. When she got to the restaurant, Cassie and Zoe were already there, seated at a table for four near the back of the room. Meg slipped off her coat and hung it on the back of the black metal chair next to where Cassie sat.

"Hey, Meg." Zoe held up a tortilla chip coated in cheese sauce and gestured with her chin at an oval plate piled high with nachos. Specks of red pepper and spicy taco meat clung to the creamy yellow cheese, punctuated by rings of bright green onion. "Feel free to take some. Their portions are huge!"

Cassie groaned. "I'm pretty sure these aren't on my diet." She lifted a chip and stuck it in her mouth anyway. "They're so good though."

Meg laughed and dug in. "You don't have to tell me twice. I'm always starving after work."

"You work in a restaurant," Zoe pointed out. "How are you hungry?"

"Yeah, but it's like the cobbler's son not having any

shoes. I'm smelling yummy food all night, but I don't have any time to eat." Meg finished chewing and picked up the menu. "Are there any specials tonight? I always like to try the new stuff."

"You'd have to ask the waitress," Cassie said. "I already ordered a cheeseburger and fries. I'm not one to mess with a classic."

The waitress came over to their table, and Meg placed her order for the fried local oysters, which the waitress assured her was the best thing on the menu that day.

"Excuse me," Cassie said to the waitress. "Can I have a glass of Chardonnay please?"

The waitress nodded and hurried off to the next table.

"It's been a long day," Cassie said. "I finished up a cake and brought it to my client, then popped in to see Celia." She cast a glance at Zoe. "And I finally met the famous Shawn. I see what you like about him."

Zoe's cheeks turned pink. "Oh? Did you have a chance to talk with him? Did he tell you about Celia?"

Cassie nodded. "He told me she's his grandmother."

Meg sat up. This was news to her. "Grandmother? But Celia doesn't have any kids. I've known her since I was a baby. How could I not have heard about this before?"

Zoe shrugged. "I don't know much about it, other than what he told me when I saw him last night, but apparently, she's his mother's birth mother." Her expression turned troubled. "I hope she wakes up soon."

"Me too," Meg said. "It's killing my grandma to be in Arizona right now, but she hates flying with a passion and doesn't want to drive back up here yet." She eyed Zoe. "Do you think Grandma knew about Celia's daughter?"

"I think she had an inkling," Zoe said carefully. "She knew enough to tell me to call Shawn when Celia had her accident."

"I'm sure Celia's going to be fine," Cassie said. "She just needs a little time for her brain to heal."

"I hope so." Zoe sipped her glass of iced tea. "I need to talk to her about a few things going on with the Inn."

Cassie turned to Meg, "Hey, your mom said I could use her catering kitchen for my cake business, at least for the near future."

"Oh good. Zoe mentioned it to me yesterday, but I hadn't had a chance to ask her about it yet." Meg drank deeply from the glass of water the waitress had brought her. Although it had been cool outside, Pondera Bistro was over a mile from the Lodge, and she'd mindlessly speed-walked the entire way.

"That's great," Zoe said. "I'm sure something will come up for use later." She wrinkled her nose. "Or maybe Lara will move back to wherever she was before she came back to Willa Bay. That would solve a lot of problems."

"No kidding." Meg frowned. "I'm sorry all of this has been happening to you guys. I can't believe how much havoc Lara's return has caused in the last two weeks."

"I know." Zoe sighed and stared at her plate. "I've actually been thinking of leaving the Lodge and finding a new job."

Meg's head shot up, and she dropped her hand away from the chip she'd been reaching for. "Leaving?"

"Yeah. It's crazy at work now. When Joan leaves, I won't even have her around to act as a buffer between Pearson and me."

Meg looked from one friend to the other. "One of my former co-workers in Portland called to tell me about a possible job there."

"Ooh," Cassie said. "That's so exciting!" Then, her lips turned downward. "But we'd miss you if you left. When you lived in Portland, I only saw you once a year."

Zoe didn't say anything but eyed Meg thoughtfully.

"I don't know if I even want to interview for it." Meg's stomach twisted. "I like living here, but ..."

"But there's room to grow in Portland," Zoe finished Meg's sentence.

Meg nodded. "If I stay here, I'll always be Taylor's assistant. I'll never get to achieve my dream of having a restaurant of my own."

"It sounds like you've got a lot to think about," Cassie said.

The waitress brought their food, and all three women dug in. Meg was glad for the reprieve from thinking about the possibility of moving away from her family and friends again. It might be the best thing for her career, but was it the best thing for her overall?

16

Shawn

The rustling of nurses and doctors running into Celia's hospital room jolted Shawn awake. He bolted upright and blinked his eyes a few times to clear the haze. After spending most of the day working on shoring up the old decking at the Inn, he'd been exhausted and had dozed off while sitting next to Celia. Now he was wide awake, trying to figure out what was going on.

One of the nurses was fiddling with Celia's monitor, while another was taking her pulse by hand. A doctor stood off to the side, taking notes on her tablet while she waited for them to finish. This was the most crowded Shawn had seen Celia's room in the week he'd been visiting her. Had something happened?

Shawn's gaze slid over to Celia, and his breath caught. Her eyes were open. Beautiful dark-blue eyes, a mirror image of his mother's.

"Celia?" He stared at her, almost forgetting the medical professionals in the room.

Her eyelids fluttered down, as if struggling to stay open, but a smile spread across her face.

"Mrs. James, we're so glad to see you're awake." The doctor beamed at her.

Celia's eyes snapped open and darted around the room wildly. "Whu—" she tried to say.

The doctor put a hand on her upper arm. "You had a little fall, but we've been taking good care of you in the hospital."

Shawn's heart clenched at the confusion on Celia's face. He wrapped his hand over the top of hers like he had so many times before, but this time, she squeezed back.

A nurse helped Celia to drink some water. It dribbled down her chin, and the nurse wiped it away with a cloth.

"What happened? Why am I in the hospital?" Celia asked.

The doctor and nurses turned to Shawn to allow him to explain. He felt odd telling her what had happened, since they'd never met before, and he hadn't been the one to discover her the day she fell.

"Your neighbor, Zoe, found you on the floor of your living room. She said it looked like you'd tried to reach for something and fell over." He watched her face. "You apparently hit your head and have been unconscious."

She touched her scalp, and the confusion stayed on her face. "My head?"

He nodded. "That was about nine days ago, so it's mostly healed now."

The doctor intervened. "You broke your hip and femur in the fall as well, but we've patched you up."

Celia glanced at her left leg and winced. "It hurts."

"That's to be expected," the doctor said. "You'll need some time in a rehabilitation center before you gain full mobility in that leg. The pain should lessen with each day though."

Her lips trembled, and she blinked her eyes. "I'm feeling a little tired now."

"That's fine, Mrs. James." The doctor smiled at her. "We'll leave you alone to get some rest. Things will be better in the morning. All of us here are so happy to see you awake though." She ushered the two nurses out of the room, then turned to Shawn. "Please let us know if Mrs. James needs anything."

"I will," he said, although Celia had closed her eyes and already appeared to be asleep.

The doctor left and Shawn got up from his chair. He walked over to the window and stared at the freshly plowed fields outside. He'd been waiting for Celia to awaken, but now what? Did she have any idea who he was? She'd eyed him with confusion, so maybe not. If she woke up again while he was there, should he say something about her being his biological grandmother? It seemed like a lot to toss at someone who'd just come out of a coma.

With a start, he realized he needed to let Zoe know that Celia was awake. He quickly dialed her number and waited for her to pick up.

"Hello," she said brightly.

Hearing her voice calmed him and made him feel like everything was going to be okay. It surprised him that someone he'd known for less than two weeks could have such a strong effect on him. "Hey, Zoe. I'm at the hospital—"

She cut him off, terror in her voice. "Is Celia okay?"

"Yes." Joy bubbled up from deep inside of him, breaking the tension he'd felt since arriving in Willa Bay. "Better than okay. She's awake."

"She is?" Zoe asked excitedly. "Should I come up and see her?"

"Um," he looked over at Celia, who was still out. "It might be better to come tomorrow. She was only awake for a few minutes, but I think it was all a little much for her. She's sleeping now."

"Okay, if you think that's best, I'll wait until tomorrow." She sighed in relief. "I'm so glad she's going to be okay."

"Me too." He sat down beside Celia. Now that she'd reached consciousness, it was becoming real. He had a grandmother he'd never known.

"Did she recognize you?" Zoe asked.

"I'm not sure," he said. "She looked at me, but she was so confused about everything. I'm not sure she even realized where she was or why she was here. The doctor seemed to think she'd feel better by tomorrow though."

"This will be odd for her." Zoe was quiet for a moment. "I can't imagine how difficult it must have been to know about you and your sister for so long, but not feel like she could make contact with you."

"Yeah." Both sets of his grandparents had died before he was a teenager, and he missed them every day. He didn't want to be angry with his mother for hiding Celia from him for his whole life, but it seemed unfair to have missed out on so many years with his biological grandmother. He took a deep breath. All of that was behind them now, and he intended to make up for lost time with Celia.

~

Celia

. . .

In the middle of the night, Celia woke up and stared at the ceiling, slowly remembering where she was and why she was there. Earlier, waking to find herself in an unknown bed, hooked up to machines with strangers surrounding her had been the most terrifying experience of her life. She still wasn't sure how she'd ended up there, although she had a vague recollection of knocking the remote off the end of the table and thinking she needed to pick it up. After that, everything went blank.

And that man who'd been sitting next to her – the one who didn't seem to be hospital staff – who had that been? He'd known how she fell, and he'd mentioned Zoe. He looked so much like her first love, Artie, that she wanted to believe it was Shawn.

But that was crazy. What would her grandson be doing in Willa Bay? She tried to push herself up to a seated position, but was still too weak to do so.

A thought came to her: Elizabeth. Her old friend was the only one who knew about Andrea and her kids. She would have known to tell Zoe about Shawn.

Celia melted into the pillows. Had that been Shawn? And if so, did he know the truth about who she really was? The last address she'd had for him was in Charleston, South Carolina. Would he have come out to Washington, just to see her – especially not knowing anything about her?

And what about Pebbles? An image of the dear little dog who'd been her constant companion for the last few years flashed through her head. Who was taking care of him? Would they be willing to continue doing so for the next few months that she'd be stuck in a convalescent home?

Realizations came crashing into her mind like a runaway freight train. Maintaining the Inn and the surrounding grounds was difficult enough when she was living there. How would she manage everything if she was away from it for a long while? An even worse thought occurred to her – the property taxes. If she didn't figure out a solution for paying those soon, she wouldn't have a home to return to by the time she'd recovered.

Her chest tightened and the machine next to her started beeping loudly. A nurse ran into the room, her rubber-bottomed shoes slapping noisily against the linoleum floor. A second nurse followed close behind her.

"Are you okay, Mrs. James?" The first nurse turned on the overhead light to supplement the corner light left on all the time so they could see when they made rounds in the middle of the night. The machine had stopped beeping, but Celia's stress levels were still through the roof.

She nodded, but it took all of her energy to do so. "I'm okay."

The second nurse examined a printout that she pulled from the machine. "It looks like your heart rate shot up suddenly. Did something happen?" She wrapped a wide blue cuff around Celia's arm.

Celia shook her head and croaked out, "I woke up and worked myself up worrying about everything."

The nurse smiled at her and checked the readout on the cuff. "It looks like it's coming down now. Try not to worry so much. You've got a great support system."

Celia's eyebrows knit together in confusion. What was she talking about? "Support system?"

"Yeah. All of your friends. There has almost always been at least one person in here with you, even though you've been here for over a week. They wanted to make sure someone would be here when you woke up." The nurse wound up the blood pressure cuff and tucked it into the side of the machine next to Celia's bed.

A warmth ran through Celia's body, calming her worries. Shawn, Zoe, and the other girls must have been visiting her while she was unconscious. How had they had time for that? She knew they cared about her, but how had they managed to fit in hospital visits with everything else going on in their busy lives?

"It looks like you're doing better now, Mrs. James." The nurse patted Celia's arm, which lay on top of the crisp, white hospital sheets. "Try to get some sleep."

Celia nodded, and the nurse turned off the overhead light and left the room. Celia thought she'd have trouble falling asleep again in the unfamiliar place, but soon she was drifting in and out of consciousness, her thoughts full of gratitude and hope for the future.

17

Zoe

Zoe lounged in the hard plastic chair, flipping through the pages of a magazine to kill time. She'd woken up with the sun that morning and driven straight to the hospital to be there when Celia woke up, in case her friend was still confused. Celia's legs rustled under the sheets, drawing Zoe's attention. "Hey, you're awake."

"Hello," Celia said, her voice gravelly with sleep and lack of use. Her eyes opened slowly, coming to rest on Zoe.

Zoe blinked back tears. It was good to hear her friend talking again. "We missed you."

Celia smiled softly at her. "I missed all of you too." She pushed against the mattress with her hands to sit up, and Zoe helped her raise the bed and put pillows behind her back. "The nurses tell me that I was in a coma for over a week." She shook her head. "I don't remember much of it at all."

"Well, not much has happened in that week." Zoe grinned at her. A lot had happened over the last ten days, but she certainly wasn't going to tell Celia about everything going on at the Lodge. "Except maybe with Pebbles – he's developed a fondness for the beach."

Celia laughed. "It's been a while since I was able to get down to the beach. Those steps ..."

"Actually, about the steps," Zoe said. "Shawn's been working on a few things at your house, and he fixed the steps to the beach. When you get back home, you'll be able to take Pebbles on all the beach walks he wants."

Celia eyed her leg ruefully. "Sounds like it's going to be a while before I walk anywhere on my own. The doctor said I'll be moved to a rehabilitation center tomorrow."

"But after that, you can come home." Zoe tried to make her voice as positive as possible for Celia's benefit.

"I hope so." Celia peered at Zoe. "So that *was* Shawn who was here?"

"Yes. When you had your accident, the hospital would only let your official emergency contact make decisions about your care. I wasn't sure who to call, but Elizabeth Arnold told me to find his phone number in your address book."

"I figured as much," Celia nodded. "Does he know who I am?" she added quietly.

Zoe wasn't sure how much to tell her. Shawn had opted to let Celia have the day after she woke up to recover before visiting. "Yes. He knows you're his grandmother."

Celia sucked in her breath, then let it out slowly. "Good. I'm glad he knows." She looked around the room. "Do you think he'll be by to see me?"

"He's planning on being here tonight. He didn't want his presence to upset you," Zoe said.

"It won't upset me." Celia gestured to a glass of water

the nurse had set on her bedside tray. "Could you please help me with that?"

"Of course." Zoe lifted the glass and guided the straw into Celia's mouth.

"Thank you," she said when she was done drinking. She scrutinized Zoe's face. "I hate to ask since you've already done so much for me, but could you check through my mail to see if there are bills or anything else important in there?"

Zoe was glad Celia had brought up her mail, because it had started to pile up – and after finding the notification of a late tax payment, Zoe wasn't sure what she'd find in there. "Sure. I can do that." She hesitated for a few seconds, unsure of how Celia would react to her next question. Finally, she blurted out, "Would you mind if Shawn and I figure out what work needs to be done to the Inn while you're gone? He's a good carpenter and is between projects. I think he'd love to help you out."

Celia pressed her lips together and inhaled deeply through her nose. "I can't afford to pay him." She looked close to tears at the admission.

"I don't think he expects any payment. He's happy to help you." Zoe had anticipated that this wouldn't be an easy topic to discuss with Celia. The elderly woman hadn't gotten any less stubborn after her accident. "Anything that he can't do himself, we'll put on a list to discuss later." Zoe checked her watch. "I have an appointment to get to right now, but I'll be back tonight."

"Oh." Celia's face fell. "I was hoping you'd stay a while."

Zoe smiled and stood. "I can't monopolize your time like that – you've got a full roster of friends who are excited to spend time with you today. In fact, I think I hear Debbie in the hallway right now."

Debbie's voice floated into the room from where she was chatting with someone at the nurses station.

Zoe had contacted everyone to let them know that Celia was awake, and they'd sprang into action with a plan to keep her company for the daytime hours. Debbie had the first shift while Zoe met Shawn at the Inn to determine what maintenance was needed.

Now that Celia was awake, with a three-month-long stay in a rehabilitation center in her future, decisions needed to be made about the Inn. Zoe wanted to do everything she could to ensure that it was a safe place for Celia to return home to.

She heard the door open and gently patted Celia's shoulder. "I'll see you later. Have fun with the girls."

Celia nodded. "Thank you, dear – for everything."

Zoe smiled as Debbie breezed into the room, and Celia's eyes lit up at the sight of her.

"Celia." Debbie leaned down to give the older woman a hug. "I'm so glad you're okay."

"It's good to see you." Celia motioned to the chair next to her that Zoe had just vacated. "Have a seat and let's catch up."

Zoe took one last look at Celia and left the room smiling.

Later, when Zoe arrived at the Inn, Shawn met her at the front door with a cup of hot coffee. Pebbles bounced around their feet, nearly tripping her as she entered the house.

"Thanks." She accepted the coffee from him and wrapped her hands around the ceramic mug, savoring its warmth. The sun was out, but it would take another few hours before the damp, chilly morning became only a distant memory.

"You're welcome." He grinned at her. "I figure we have

a long day ahead of us." He glanced around the entry hall. "From what I've seen, Celia's been deferring maintenance on this place for years."

"Yeah. And unfortunately, it doesn't sound like she has the funds to fix it. She was worried about paying you for the work you've already done." Zoe sipped her coffee. He'd made it stronger than most people would, but it was just the way she liked it.

Shawn looked up at the ceiling and sighed loudly. "I don't want her to pay me back. I want to help her."

Zoe held up her hand. "Don't worry, I already told her you don't expect any payment, but I have to warn you – she's stubborn."

He shook his head. "She doesn't owe me anything. I don't know why she gave my mother up for adoption, but I'm sure she had her reasons. If she wants to be part of my life, I'd love to be part of hers."

They walked into the kitchen, and Shawn refilled his cup. "This kitchen is badly in need of new flooring, a new dishwasher, and updated plumbing, at the very least. I've tried repairing the sink, but it's all rusting out."

"Okay." Zoe grabbed the notebook and pen she'd brought with her to track all of the repairs. "I have no clue how she's going to pay for any of this, but let's get a full inventory of what should be done and what is absolutely necessary for her to return home."

They toured the rest of the main floor, with Shawn inspecting everything in the living room, sitting room, and downstairs owner's suite that Celia used as her bedroom. By the time they were ready to tour the upstairs, Zoe had already filled three pages with notes.

"Ready?" Shawn asked.

Zoe nodded. "I've never been up there, and I'm curious to see what it looks like."

"I've been camping out in one of the rooms, but things up there are rough. Watch your step, because some of the carpet treads aren't glued down very well anymore, and the railing is coming loose in a few spots." He started up the stairs, and Zoe followed behind him.

When they got to the top, Zoe stopped to take in her surroundings. Six doors lined each side of a long, dark hallway, with a seventh at the end. Only the first door on the left was open, allowing a wide beam of light to illuminate the space. She assumed it led to the bedroom Shawn was using.

"It's bigger than I expected," Zoe said.

"Bigger means more work." Shawn grimaced. "There are two bathrooms up here, but I don't think they've been used in the last decade."

"Only two?" she asked. "So, there are ten bedrooms and two bathrooms?" Although they'd been built around the same time, every room in Willa Bay Lodge had ensuite bathrooms, but they'd been added at a later date to satisfy guest preferences. Evidently, Celia and her husband Charlie had never felt the need to modernize their accommodations.

"Here's the first of them." He pushed open a door midway down the right side of the hallway. A dank odor of mildew wafted through the air.

"Eww." Zoe wrinkled up her nose.

"Yeah. The other one's even worse. The walls and floor all need to be replaced." He closed the door tightly. "Want to see it?"

"Thanks, but I'll take your word for it." She wrote down the number of bathrooms and made a note about their condition. "Let's move on to the bedrooms."

He shrugged and went to the open door. "You can see

where I've been staying. I've got it cleaned up a bit, so it shows better than the rest of them."

She was curious to see what his bedroom looked like. He motioned for her to enter in front of him. The double bed was neatly made, with the sheets and blankets tucked tightly under the mattress and two pillows propped against the scarred wooden headboard. The closet door was shut, most likely containing his suitcase and other belongings. A framed photo of two adults sat on top of the dresser. Other than the photo, which Zoe assumed was of his parents, there was no indication of who lived in the room.

She walked around the foot of the bed to look out the window. Below, the freshly cut lawn gleamed with dew as it rolled down to the gazebo, ending high above the sparkling blue waters of Willa Bay. "The view from here is gorgeous. I'm not surprised the Inn was popular back in the day." She noticed a water spot on the wallpaper and traced the leak up to the ceiling, where an irregular shape the length of a large watermelon hung overhead. "Is the roof leaking?"

"I hope it isn't anymore." He scrutinized the water damage. "I've patched the roof as best as I can, but it really needs to be completely replaced. It looked like it had already been patched several times over the years. In fact, I'd say that was the number one item on my list of things that absolutely need to get fixed around here."

She wrote "FIX ROOF" at the top of a page. "Are there other places where it's leaked?"

"Every room up here has some sort of water damage. I'll show you." He took her through the rest of the rooms, and as he pointed out the flaws in each, her hopefulness plummeted. There was already so much inside the Inn to repair. They hadn't even gotten to the grounds or exterior maintenance. And fixing up the cottages? That was never going to happen at this rate.

Shawn started to descend the staircase with Zoe following closely behind him. She ran her hand along the railing as she went, keeping in mind his warning about the loose carpet treads. When she was midway down the stairs, however, her left foot caught on the corner of a piece of carpet, and she lost her balance. She clutched for the railing attached to the wall, but it gave way under her weight, catapulting her forward.

Hearing the clatter behind him, Shawn pivoted quickly and caught her with one arm, grabbing a stable portion of the railing with the other hand. He cradled her close to his chest, his eyes mere inches away from hers as he searched her face. "Are you okay?"

Zoe clung to him for a moment without answering, one hand grasping him tightly around the neck and the other resting on his bicep, which strained under her fingers as he gripped the railing to support them. She peered past him down the steep flight of stairs. If he hadn't caught her, she would have sustained a nasty injury in the fall.

She shivered and leaned against him. Warmth radiated through his thin T-shirt, calming her nerves – and at the same time, reminding her how close she was to him. Her pulse quickened as she met his gaze. "I think so. Thank you for catching me."

"You're welcome." Shawn released Zoe, steadying her on the stair above him. He stared at the railing hanging uselessly on one end by a single screw and shook his head. "You could have been hurt. I should have prioritized fixing those railings."

Zoe forced a small smile. She hated that he blamed himself for her mishap. "It's okay – I'm fine. You've been working on so many other important projects around here. If it hadn't been this particular railing, it could have just as easily been one on the deck. This place is an accident waiting to happen." She cringed, thinking of Celia's recent fall.

Doubt pooled in his eyes. "Still – you could have been hurt. Fixing these stairs needs to move to the top of my list."

She took a deep breath. "Speaking of that list – we'd better check out the rest of the property." Although, after what she'd seen upstairs, she wasn't sure she wanted to see the condition of everything else.

He nodded, briefly caressing her arm before turning away from her, as if confirming she was really okay. Zoe's legs trembled as she made her way down to the main floor. She'd come close to falling from halfway up a flight of stairs. If Shawn hadn't caught her ... She forced the thought out of her mind. He *had* been there.

"This is depressing," Zoe said as they went outside. She took a deep breath of the salty air, hoping it would fortify her as they looked at the exterior of the house. She already knew it was in rough shape.

Shawn scanned the side of the building. "I can already tell you that the siding needs to be repaired, the whole exterior repainted, and the rest of the porch fixed. It could use some newer, more energy-efficient windows too, but that's further down on the list."

Zoe slumped into a chair on the front porch, staring out at the bay. "So, for just the roof and the smaller plumbing jobs like the kitchen sink, how much is this going to cost?"

His brow furrowed as he thought. "I'd say at least twenty grand – and that's if I provide some of the labor. That roof is no small job."

Her heart sank all the way to the ground. "Celia doesn't have that kind of money."

He sighed. "I wish I could help more, but I'm not rolling in dough either."

"Celia needs to come home to the Inn." Zoe knew if Celia was forced to live in a retirement home long-term, she'd wither and die there.

"Zoe ..." Shawn took a deep breath. "I don't think Celia's going to be able to come back to the Inn. It's just not feasible. She's got that huge tax bill and all of the necessary repairs on top of it. I know you want to help her, but it's just not going to work."

"There has to be a way." Zoe lifted her chin.

"There's not," he said gently. "Unless Celia has some sort of fairy godmother or a stash of cash somewhere that we don't know about, the best we can do for her is to get this place ready to sell."

"You don't understand. This is Celia's home. She has to come back here." Why couldn't Shawn understand how important it was for Celia to be in her own home?

"We're going to have to tell her that we know about the tax situation and that she needs to sell the property. She's not going to live here."

Zoe clenched her jaw so tightly that her teeth ached. "You can't tell her that."

He sighed. "We can live in la-la land for now and work on fixing up the property, but you're going to have to be honest with her eventually."

"Fine." She glared at him. "But I'm going to figure out a way to make this work."

"Okay." He shrugged resignedly. "But until then, I'm going to operate on the assumption that Celia will be selling this place." He leaned against one of the porch posts that he'd recently replaced. "Look, I don't want to fight about this. All I want is for us to be honest with each other and with Celia about the status of the property. I don't think it will work for her to keep it, but I'll be happy to have you prove me wrong."

"I will." A fire burned in Zoe from head to toe. When she latched on to a project or idea, she was like a dog with a bone. Nothing else in her life was going right, but she could do something about this.

He ran a hand over his hair. "I'll call the county assessor and see if we can put off the tax sale, but I doubt they'll drop the matter indefinitely. You're going to need to figure out how to pay them."

She nodded. Shawn obviously didn't believe that they could pull off saving the Inn, but she was going to accept his challenge and prove him wrong.

18

Cassie

Cassie walked into the Lodge at five o'clock in the morning, enjoying the peace and quiet. At this time of day, only one person ran the front desk, and she was engrossed in reading a newspaper. Outside, Cassie had encountered a young couple jogging, but other than that, everyone else was still asleep in their beds.

Sometimes Cassie missed getting to sleep in later, but she also relished the solitude of an early morning. There was nothing more luxurious than pulling a fresh loaf of bread from the oven with no one else around to steal the heel. This morning, however, something was different. She sensed it as soon as she entered the staff hallway leading to the kitchen.

The mixer was running. Its low vibrations would be almost imperceptible to most but were easily identifiable to her. She quickened her pace. Why was the mixer on?

She pushed open the door and stepped onto the tiled kitchen floor. A woman with blonde streaks in her brown hair stood in front of the mixer, shutting it off just as Cassie entered.

The woman looked up at Cassie and frowned. "Oh. It's you."

Cassie stopped short. "Lara. What are you doing here?" Cassie's eyes traveled across the kitchen counters and over to the oven, which had its preheat indicator lit. The place had been trashed since she'd left the day before. What was going on?

Lara rolled her eyes with the disdain of a teenager. "I'm baking a cake. What does it look like?"

Cassie slowly counted to three in her mind, just like when she was in the middle of a "talk" with one of her kids and didn't want to blow up at them. "Okay. Why are you baking a cake here?" Not to mention, why was she there at five in the morning?

"I'm using the facilities at the Lodge until I can get my own bakery." Lara grabbed the bowl from the mixer and poured the dark batter into the first of three round cake pans she'd already greased and floured. "What's your hurry anyway? I should be done in a couple of hours. I didn't figure anyone would be here until eight or so."

Counting to three wasn't cutting it this time. Cassie leaned against the counter, gripping the edges of it until they bit into her hands. "I need the kitchen to prepare the breakfast breads," she said. "I get here early so I can get everything done before the guests wake up."

Lara looked around. "Well, you should have plenty of room to work. I'm not taking up *that* much space."

Cassie eyed the flour spilled all over the floor, the cartons of eggs lying open on the counter, and the measuring cups strewn about. Lara had somehow managed to spill crimson food dye on the white floor tiles, making it look like someone had been murdered in the middle of the kitchen. If Taylor saw the mess Lara had made, there *would* be a murder in the kitchen. He thrived on cleanliness and order and wouldn't be pleased with the current state of his domain.

Cassie's lips twitched, and she bit back a smile.

"What's so funny?" Lara snapped. She picked up one of the cake pans and set it in the oven, then returned to the counter for the next.

"Oh, nothing." Cassie gestured to the powdering of flour and red streaks on the floor. "But you might want to get this taken care of before Taylor comes in for the day."

Lara scoffed. "I'm sure the kitchen staff will take care of it when they get here. I'm not too worried about what Taylor will think." She laughed. "Besides, my father owns the place. What can Taylor possibly do to me?"

Cassie stared at her, unused to seeing this kind of entitlement – even out of her own kids, who definitely had their moments. She spun on her heel and left the kitchen before she could say anything she'd regret later.

An hour later, Cassie returned to the kitchen hoping Lara had wised up and cleaned it. Time was running out to make the breakfast breads, but if Cassie started now, she could accomplish half of what she'd planned to make.

If anything, the kitchen was worse. Lara had taken the cakes out of the oven to cool and had set them on one of the few clean surfaces. Without a word to her, Cassie cleaned and sanitized a workspace and made her famous cinnamon raisin rolls, along with some blueberry scones. When they were in the oven, she cleaned up her own mess, but left the rest of Lara's alone.

By eight o'clock, the kitchen was heavily scented with a spicy-sweet cinnamon aroma that soothed Cassie's soul. She'd managed to avoid talking to Lara the whole time – a fairly amazing accomplishment considering they were working within ten feet of each other.

"Cassie," a woman called out from the door to the staff hallway. "Do you have any more cookies for the front desk?"

Drat. She hadn't made extra cookies the day before, because she'd been intending to try out a new snickerdoodle recipe in the morning. That had all gone out the window when she found Lara invading her space.

"I'm sorry. I don't have any right now. I'll get something going and bring them out to you." Cassie hurried to mix up a batch of peanut butter cookies, an old standby with a recipe she knew by heart.

When they were ready, Lara was frosting the cakes she'd stacked atop each other. With any luck, she'd be out of there soon. On the way back from delivering the cookies to the front desk, Cassie stopped in front of George's closed office door. She steeled herself with a quick mental pep talk, then rapped on the door.

"Come in."

She turned the doorknob and stepped inside his office, closing the door behind her. "George, I need to talk to you about something."

"Sure, Cassie, what is it?" He pushed his chair back and peered at her through his thick glasses.

"I need to talk to you about Lara."

His bushy eyebrows rose a half of an inch. "Lara?"

Cassie took a deep breath. "She was in the kitchen early this morning when I came in to bake."

He smiled. "Ah, yes. I told her she could use the kitchen in the mornings."

"But I need it in the mornings – otherwise I can't get everything done in time for the guests to have freshly baked goods for breakfast."

"Oh. I see." He tented his hands and lifted his fingertips up to his chin. "It's a big kitchen though. There should be plenty of room for both of you, right? I realize this must be a little awkward, but I'm sure the two of you can get along."

She stared at him. How could she tell him that his daughter had taken over the kitchen and made a huge mess which she refused to clean up? That was a sure-fire way to get fired, and Cassie couldn't afford to lose her job.

She forced a smile. "Yes. I'm sure we can make it work. I just wanted to check with you first. I'd better get back to work." She rushed out of the office and closed the door quietly behind her. There wasn't much of a choice – she'd have to figure out how to work alongside Lara if she wanted to keep her job at the Lodge.

Lara finally left around ten, and Cassie set about cleaning the kitchen before Meg and Taylor arrived for the lunch rush. By the time they got there, everything was sparkling. She didn't bother telling them that a few hours earlier, the kitchen looked like a toddler had been set loose in it.

As soon as the clock struck two, Cassie threw her apron on the hook and practically ran out to the parking lot. More than anything, she wanted a few moments alone to regroup before her kids came home from school. Unfortunately, Kyle was sitting on her porch when she drove up.

"Hi," Cassie said, jangling her keys. "I didn't expect to see you here yet. The kids won't be home for another hour." Jace was supposed to build a working volcano for school, and he'd asked for his dad to come over and help with it. Jace was so excited about the science project that Cassie didn't have the heart to say no to his request.

"I know. I was hoping to talk with you first," Kyle said.

"Oh?" She unlocked the front door and gestured for him to come inside. "What about?"

"Now that tax season is over, I was hoping to have the kids over at my place more often. Would that be okay with you?" His tone was more considerate than she'd heard from him in a long time.

"That would be fine. I could use the extra time anyway. I need to find a new place for my cake decorating business." She set her purse and keys on a side table and hung her coat up on a hook on the wall.

Kyle followed her into the kitchen. "I thought your boss at the Lodge was letting you use the kitchen there."

"He was, until his daughter moved back home to Willa Bay and decided she wanted to be a cake decorator. She needed the space, so I'm out of luck." Cassie filled a glass with iced tea out of the fridge and sank into a chair at the kitchen table.

"Oh, Cassie, I'm sorry." Kyle frowned. "Is there anything I can do?"

Cassie started laughing. "Well, can you figure out how to make Lara Camden go back to wherever she was living before she moved home? Because that would solve a lot of my problems." Cassie laughed uncontrollably until she cried, so overcome with stress that she didn't know how to feel.

Kyle sat at the end of the table next to her, a stricken expression on his face. "Are you okay?"

"I'm fine." She hiccupped and grabbed a Kleenex from the box on the table. "I just feel like everything is falling apart. My life wasn't supposed to be this way. You and I were supposed to be happily married forever with our two perfect kids, leading the ideal life." She laughed again, and his face registered alarm.

"Seriously, Cass, is there anything I can do to help?"

She wiped away a stray tear, then looked down at the table. "I don't know," she whispered.

He scooted his chair closer and wrapped his arm around her shoulders. Normally, she would have recoiled at his touch, but right now, she welcomed the familiar weight of his arm around her. She leaned into him. "I'm failing, and I don't know what to do."

He gave her shoulders a squeeze and released her, lifting her chin tenderly before gazing deeply into her eyes. "I know things between us haven't gone as planned, but you're the mother of my children, and I'll always be here for you, okay?"

She nodded.

"Now, what can we do to make things better for you? I'm going to take the kids more so you can focus on work, but I'm not sure the Lodge is a good place for you anymore." He searched her face. "Do you even want to work there?"

Her shoulders slumped. "I don't have much of a choice. The schedule is perfect for me with the kids, and I've always enjoyed it in the past. But now that Lara is there, things are just going to get worse."

"So quit." He sighed and leaned back in his chair. "You're an amazing baker, and I'm sure you'll find a job in no time. In the meantime, I can help you out with the money part of it."

It was like she was in the Twilight Zone or something. Who was this kind and understanding man sitting in front of her?

"Thank you," she said. "I truly appreciate it. I'm going to try to stick it out at the Lodge, but I'll let you know if things change."

The front door opened, and the kids walked in from school.

"Dad?" Jace shouted. "I saw your car outside. Are you here?"

Kyle and Cassie exchanged amused glances, and she hurriedly wiped her face.

"In here," Kyle called back.

Amanda came into the kitchen to let them know she was going to her room to do her homework.

"Can we start on the volcano now?" Jace bounced up and down on the balls of his feet.

"Yep." Cassie walked over to the kitchen counter and moved all of the necessary items for the project over to the table, then sat down to work on it with Jace and Kyle. An hour later, she left to check on Amanda. When she came back, she stopped in the entrance to the kitchen, memorizing the sight of her son and ex-husband's heads crowded close together as they read the instructions for the next step in building a model volcano.

Before the divorce, Kyle hadn't taken much interest in the kids, but now, he was actually trying. Perhaps there was something to the old saying "absence makes the heart grow fonder."

"Hey, guys, what can I help with now?" she asked as she joined them again at the table.

They gave her a task, and the three of them worked together on the project for the rest of the afternoon. It was like they were the happy, normal family she knew didn't really exist, but yearned for just the same.

19

Meg

When Meg arrived at work early Friday afternoon, the counters in the Lodge's kitchen were powdered with a layer of flour, and sparkling sugar formed a trail across the ceramic tiles in front of one of the prep tables. Cassie was sweeping up the mess with furious swipes of a nylon broom.

"What happened here?" Meg asked Cassie. "Did you forget to put the lid on the mixer or something?" Meg grinned at her friend, knowing full well that Cassie didn't usually use a lid on the mixer, but they liked to poke fun of each other's relative lack of knowledge of their own culinary niche.

Cassie glared at her. "No."

"Whoa." Meg stepped back to regard Cassie. "What's got your knickers in a bunch today?"

Cassie stopped sweeping and leaned on the broom. "My knickers are just fine, thank you. But Lara's won't be if she keeps leaving these messes."

"Lara did this?" Meg surveyed the disaster zone. "Wait, has she done this before?"

Cassie nodded; her face full of misery. "This is the third time this week. She thinks we have some kitchen crew that will come in and clean up after her." With a few long strokes, she swept all of the sugar into a pile.

Meg sighed. "I'm sorry, Cassie. She shouldn't be doing this. Have you talked with George about it?"

Cassie snorted. "Ha! Like he'll do anything about his daughter causing trouble. No. I talked to him about her being here when I need the space for actual Lodge baking, and he brushed off my concerns."

"Maybe it would help if I said something to him?" Meg asked as she held the dustpan in place for Cassie to sweep the debris into.

"I doubt it." Cassie placed the broom back in the utility closet attached to the kitchen and returned with two small, white cleaning cloths. She brushed off the countertop with a dry one, depositing the flour into a garbage can waiting below the lip of the counter.

Meg took the other cloth, sprayed the cleared surface with disinfectant, and wiped it down. "She can't keep doing this."

Cassie shrugged. "She's the owner's daughter." She smiled at Meg. "Let's talk about something other than Lara. Do you have any exciting weekend plans?"

"Nope. Just work here. What about you?" Meg washed her hands and put on her white chef's jacket.

"I'm taking the kids to the aquarium in Seattle with one of Amanda's friends and her mom." Cassie glanced at the clock. "I'd better get going if I want to be home before the kids."

"Have fun," Meg said. Spending hours at the

aquarium with three kids didn't seem like a good time to her, but Cassie seemed excited about it.

"Thanks. I will." Cassie grinned at her. "Have fun working."

"I will," Meg said. Cassie may have meant it sarcastically, but Meg loved what she did, and to her it *was* fun. It sometimes amazed her that she and Cassie were so different, but had been friends for over twenty years.

Cassie left, and Meg got to work prepping the ingredients for dinner. She heard the door leading to the staff hallway open and looked up to see who'd come in.

"Is Pearson here?" Zoe's eyes darted around the kitchen.

"Nope, are you looking for him?" Meg put down the paring knife she'd been using to trim the asparagus.

Zoe shook her head and entered the room, allowing the door to close softly behind her. "I'm trying to avoid him. He's driving me crazy with his cost-cutting measures. I know he's trying to make a good impression on George, but he doesn't understand what a client wants."

The door burst open, and they both stared in that direction.

"Aren't you meeting with a client now, Zoe?" Pearson asked, consulting a notebook he held in his hands.

"They called to say they'd be about ten minutes late," she said. "I'll be right out to the lobby in a minute. "I was, um ..."

"Working with me on a menu," Taylor said, as he stepped out of his office.

"Hmm." Pearson gave Zoe a side-eyed glare.

Zoe flinched, and Meg cringed at her friend's reaction. What had happened to Zoe's confidence?

"Actually, Taylor," Pearson said. "I wanted to talk to

you about our catering menus. I think we can save thousands of dollars a year if we use a different cut of meat in our entrées."

"Uh-huh." Taylor studied Pearson's face. "I'm not sure we can do that, but let's talk." He motioned to his office, and the two men went inside, shutting the door firmly behind them.

Zoe and Meg exchanged glances.

"He's awful," Meg said in a low voice. "How can you work with him?"

"I don't know." Zoe's voice was soft, as if she was close to tears. "It's only been a week and a half, and I'm about ready to quit."

"No! Don't quit." Meg hugged Zoe, but Zoe stood limply in her arms. Meg stared at her. "It's going to get better, I'm sure it will. Give it a little longer."

"I will," Zoe said. "I don't have much of a choice." Her eyes darted over to Taylor's office door. "I'm going to duck out of here while Pearson is occupied with someone else though. Maybe I can find a hidden corner of the Lodge to work in."

Meg laughed. "That's the spirit."

Zoe left the kitchen, and Meg went back to chopping vegetables for the evening's side dishes.

A few minutes later, Pearson stormed out of Taylor's office, passing Meg without a word. He flung open the door and let it slam shut behind him. Meg raised her eyebrows as she watched him go. Apparently, Pearson's meeting with Taylor hadn't gone well.

Heavy footsteps sounded on the floor behind her. "That imbecile is going to ruin this place."

Meg set down the knife and turned to face Taylor. "That bad?"

His face was flushed with anger, and his black hair

stood out in all directions, as if he'd been shoving his fingers through it. "He wants to use sirloin instead of filet mignon on our catering menu, plus he has about a thousand other 'suggestions' to make our menus more cost-efficient." He peered at her. "Have you had any interactions with him yet?"

She shook her head. "Not much, but Zoe isn't too happy with him either. He's been a tyrant to her." She leaned in and whispered, "She's thinking about quitting because he's so bad."

Taylor closed his eyes. "I don't think George understands what he's done by hiring Pearson."

A patch of flour near the base of the counter caught Meg's eye. Should she say something to Taylor about Lara? "Cassie's been cleaning up Lara's kitchen messes this week," she blurted out. "When Lara uses the kitchen for her cake business, she doesn't bother sweeping or cleaning the counters afterward. Cassie didn't want to say anything to you or George because she's worried about losing her job."

Fire burned in Taylor's eyes. Meg had always thought of him as a laid-back, California surfer-type, but right now, she wouldn't want to be the subject of his wrath.

He swallowed hard and said, "I'm going to talk to George about this right now." He stalked out of the kitchen, leaving Meg open-mouthed. Who was this guy? She had to admit, she kind of liked seeing his more passionate side.

She leaned against the counter, thinking about everything going on. Zoe was miserable at the Lodge, Cassie was worried about her job and losing her cake decorating income, and Meg had some big decisions to make, herself. Even happy-go-lucky Taylor had been driven over the edge. The one bright spot in this week was Celia waking up from her coma.

Meg turned back to the counter and moved the cut veggies into a neat pile. Thinking about everything that was wrong in her life was making her crazy. It was time to focus on moving forward.

20

Shawn

"So, what do you think of this place so far?" Shawn sat down in one of the two chairs near Celia's bed at the rehabilitation facility. Zoe sat next to him in the other chair. They'd carpooled there after having breakfast together to discuss the Inn.

Shawn hadn't known what to expect when Celia had been transferred from the hospital yesterday, but he'd been pleasantly surprised. The facility was clean and modern, and everyone he'd met there had been friendly to him and considerate with Celia. She had a roommate, who was currently out walking the halls with the physical therapist.

Celia looked around her living space. "It's fine. I can't wait to get back home though. If I never have to look at another hospital room, I'll die a happy woman."

Concern spread across Zoe's face. "But not anytime soon, I hope. We just got you back."

Celia laughed. "Nope, I intend to stay in this world for quite a while longer." She quieted. "I do miss Pebbles though. How's he doing?"

"Missing you, but settling for Zoe and I." Shawn smiled softly at Zoe. He badly wanted to talk to Celia about the state of things at the Inn, but Zoe had implored him not to say anything until Celia was settled into her temporary home.

"Shawn and I took him to the park yesterday, and he had so much fun. I think he even made a new friend," Zoe said.

"A new *girl*friend." Shawn winked at Celia. "She was a pretty little Chihuahua, and they chased each other around for at least twenty minutes."

"I bet he liked that," Celia said, a wide smile breaking out on her face. Shawn was relieved to see her smiling. He'd wondered how she'd do with the move from the hospital to the rehab center, but she seemed to be adjusting well to the change. She turned to Zoe and pointed to the dresser on the far wall, "Can you bring me my wallet, please? My purse is over there in the top drawer."

Zoe popped up from her chair. "Sure." She brought the wallet back and handed it to Celia.

Celia grasped the black leather pouch like she was going to offer them money for their help, and Shawn readied his refusal speech. Instead, however, she opened it and withdrew a well-worn photo of a young girl. She caressed the photo with her thumb before holding it out to him.

He studied the image. His dad didn't have many pictures of his mom when she was a kid, but Shawn was pretty sure this was her. "That's my mom, isn't it?" He gave it back to Celia, holding his breath as he waited for her response.

Celia nodded, her eyes glazing over with emotion as

she looked down at the image. "My cousin, Betty, sent me this when Andrea was in the fourth grade."

"You missed your daughter a lot, didn't you?" Zoe asked, not taking her eyes off Celia.

"The day I handed her over to Betty and Delbert, I lost a huge part of myself." Tears pooled in the corners of Celia's eyes, and fell freely down her wrinkled cheeks.

Shawn plucked a Kleenex from the box on the nightstand and handed it to her. "Why did you give her up?"

Celia wiped her tears away, but fresh ones rose up to take their place. "When I was twenty-five, I was engaged to be married to a wonderful man named Artie." She sighed. "We had so many plans for our future. He'd come out to Seattle for a job on the fishing boats, but he was from a little farming community in North Dakota. We hoped to buy a little farm out on the Kitsap Peninsula and raise a large family there once we were married." She sighed. "I always wanted a lot of kids."

"So, what happened with Artie?" Zoe moved to the edge of her seat.

Celia's face drooped. "He took a job on one of the crabbing boats, heading to Alaska. After months of not hearing from him, I got word that the boat he was on had gone down in a storm." She looked down at her hands, rubbing her thumbs together. "I hadn't even had a chance to tell him he was going to be a father."

"Oh," Zoe murmured. "I'm so sorry, Celia."

Celia's voice was stronger when she looked up. "After Artie died, I was so lost. When I couldn't hide the pregnancy any longer, I was let go from my job." She met Shawn's gaze. "I didn't know what to do."

He nodded, encouraging her to go on.

"An elderly aunt gave me a place to stay until I had the baby, but she barely had enough money to feed me. Staying with her after the birth wasn't an option." Celia looked past Zoe and Shawn, out the window. "But still, I wanted to keep the baby. I tried to make it work, but after she was born, I fell into a deep depression – I guess they'd call it postpartum depression nowadays, but we didn't talk much about it then. It got to the point where I felt the best option was to give the baby up to my cousin and her husband. They'd always wanted children but had never been blessed with them."

"I can't imagine how difficult that decision was for you to make." Shawn reached out and squeezed Celia's hand.

She returned his gesture with a faint smile. "It was. Giving up Andrea was the most painful moment of my entire life, even worse than finding out Artie had died in Alaska. I wanted to keep her so badly." She peered at Shawn. "I never could get your mother to believe that though."

He nodded with understanding. "She could be stubborn when she wanted to be."

"So, your cousin wouldn't let you see the baby?" Zoe's eyes were filled with unshed tears.

Celia shook her head. "No. She and her husband wanted it to be a clean break. They sent me pictures and letters throughout the years, but they requested that I not contact Andrea until she was of age." She smiled wryly. "I didn't think about the fact that I was giving up not only the baby, but what little family I had left as well. It was too hard for me to attend family events because I knew she'd be there." She sighed. "I moved up to Willa Bay and took a job as a maid at the Inn. The Olsens took me in, and over the years became a substitute family to me."

"Wow." Shawn sat back still holding on to Celia's hand. Her grip was tentative, but steady.

"Thank you for telling us about Andrea," Zoe said. "This can't be easy for you."

"It's not." Celia's gaze focused on Shawn. "But having the chance at a relationship with Shawn and his sister makes it all worth it." She gave Shawn's hand a squeeze, then pulled her hand out of his grasp to lay it down by her side. "If you don't mind, I think I'd like to rest a little now."

"Of course." Zoe got to her feet and leaned over to pat Celia's shoulder. "I'm heading to Candle Beach tomorrow morning for my grandfather's birthday party, but I'll stop in to see you before I leave. I'll only be gone for a few days, and Shawn will be here if you need anything."

Shawn flashed Zoe a smile. "That I will." He stood to leave, but paused at the foot of the bed and met Celia's gaze. "Is it okay if I call you Grandma?"

Celia nodded and blinked back tears. "I'd like that."

He smiled widely. "Then I'll see you later, Grandma." The word felt awkward on his tongue and would take some getting used to.

"See you later, Grandson." Celia closed her eyes, a huge grin illuminating her face.

～

Celia

Celia lifted her eyelids halfway, just enough to watch Zoe and Shawn leave her room at the rehabilitation center. Talking to Shawn about Artie and Andrea had opened the door to painful memories that she'd long ago buried – but it had brought relief as well. Although she'd loved Charlie with all of her heart, Artie had been her first real love, and she still wondered what could have been if they'd been able to raise Andrea together as a family.

What would her life have been like if Artie hadn't died and she hadn't had to give Andrea up? Would she and Artie have had more children – the large family they'd dreamed of? Would she be a farmer's wife right now, milking cows in the morning and feeding the chickens every afternoon?

Visions of Charlie and the Inn at Willa Bay entered her mind. Moving to Willa Bay had vanquished some of the sadness she felt over losing Artie, and time had helped with the postpartum depression. The Inn's grounds had been beautiful, and although she had only been the maid, she'd had a cottage to live in and been treated with respect. The Olsens hadn't had any children of their own and had taken her under their wing, eventually leaving the Inn to her when they passed.

She knew giving Andrea up for adoption had been the best decision at the time for both of them. It hadn't been an easy thing to do, but Celia's cousin Betty was a wonderful mother to Andrea and was able to provide for her in a way that Celia couldn't do at the time.

Still, though, her biggest regret was her inability to establish a relationship with Andrea when she reached adulthood. Being a part of Andrea's adult life and having the chance to know Shawn and Jessa when they were young would have been a blessing. But at least Shawn seemed receptive to a relationship with her now. She couldn't change the past, but she could appreciate everything the future held.

And if she wasn't mistaken, there was something going on between Zoe and her grandson. Celia had caught the soft looks between the two of them and the easy way they interacted with each other. She didn't know Shawn well, but she had a feeling Zoe would be good for him. Yes, the future was unknown, but Celia was looking forward to seeing how everything turned out.

21

Zoe

Zoe pulled into a parking space in front of Celia's rehabilitation center and turned off the engine but didn't get out immediately. Her car was packed for her trip to Candle Beach to celebrate her grandfather's eighty-fifth birthday, but before she could leave, she needed to have a serious talk with Celia about the future of the Inn.

It was something she'd been putting off for a while, hoping for a miracle that would save Celia's home. Unfortunately, the county had denied their request to postpone the seizure of the property for back taxes. Celia only had one more month to pay the back taxes, or she'd lose the Inn.

Shawn had been right – Celia wouldn't be returning home. Besides the taxes owed, there were the overwhelming repair and maintenance expenses. Celia couldn't afford to stay there. But how was Zoe going to tell her that?

She finally forced herself to open the door and step out onto the sunlit blacktop parking lot, then make her way inside. Celia's roommate was out again, and Zoe was grateful for the privacy. This wasn't going to be an easy conversation.

When she heard Zoe enter her room, Celia looked up from the large-print book she was reading. "Zoe! You didn't need to come see me this morning. I thought you were visiting your family this weekend."

"Hey, Celia," she said as she took her coat off and sat down in the chair next to Celia's bed. "I'm on my way there, but I wanted to see you before I left town."

"Well, I'm glad you did, but you've got a long drive ahead of you. You should get on the road." Celia peered at Zoe with worried eyes.

"I'll be fine." Zoe smiled, then took a deep breath. "Celia, I need to talk to you about something."

Celia cocked her head to the side. "Sure, what is it?"

"I'm worried about the Inn. Shawn and I found the bills from the tax assessor that you'd already opened, and another one that came after your accident." She kept her eyes on Celia, trying to judge the elderly woman's reaction. "I called the assessor's office, and they said you haven't paid your property taxes in years. That's a lot of money."

Celia looked away, toward the curtain that separated her living area from her roommate's. "I can't pay it." She rubbed her temples. "Charlie's life insurance ran out last year, and now I can only afford the bare necessities."

Zoe studied Celia's face. "Why didn't you say anything before?"

Celia shrugged. "I'm on my own. Who would have helped me?" Tears rimmed her eyes.

Zoe leaned over to hug the older woman. "That's not true at all. You have all of us: me, Meg, Cassie, Debbie, Elizabeth, Libby, and Samantha. Not to mention, you have Shawn now. And that's just a few of the people you've helped over the years. We would have been glad to give back to you if you'd only asked."

Celia looked down at her hands. "It's too late now, though, isn't it? I'm out of time and money."

Zoe sighed. "I wish I could tell you no, but we contacted the county, and they're unwilling to give you more time. You have to move out within the next month."

Celia pressed her lips together, as if trying to hold back a sob. She took a shallow breath. "But I'll still be in this place for at least a month. How will I get everything packed to move?"

"Like I said, we're here for you." Zoe patted her arm. "I'm still hoping for a miracle to save the Inn, but if it doesn't appear, all of us are here to help you."

Celia heaved a shuddering sigh, then nodded. "Thank you." She eyed the clock on the wall. "The physical therapist will be here soon to help me exercise, and you'd better get going. I don't want you to be driving there in the dark."

Zoe smiled. Celia was always thinking about someone else's needs rather than her own. "I'll be okay. But if it makes you feel better, I'll leave now. I think Shawn is planning on visiting later this afternoon."

"Enjoy your time with your family. You work so hard, and I'm glad you have a chance to get home to see them." Celia picked up the book that she'd tented over the blankets. "It's important to spend time with those you love." She gave her a brave smile. "And don't worry about me. I always knew losing the Inn was a possibility. I'll be fine."

"I know, but I still feel bad that I couldn't do more." Zoe bent down to hug her again. "I'll see you in a few days."

"See you soon." Celia lifted her book closer to her face, and Zoe left her room.

Zoe drove away from the rehabilitation center with a pit in her stomach. Celia seemed to have outwardly accepted that she'd need to move, but how did she really feel about it? Knowing how important the Inn was to Celia, Zoe had a hard time believing that she would be okay with moving.

The drive to Candle Beach passed in a blur. After being landlocked on multilane freeways and highways for much of the trip, Zoe's stress levels eased as the massive waves of the Pacific Ocean came into view. The highway mimicked the curves of the rugged shoreline as it snaked north through dense tunnels of trees and stump-littered land that had been logged within the past decade.

Zoe had arranged to have time off for her grandfather's birthday party six months ago, but Pearson had tried to cancel her vacation. She'd told him that she was not going to change her plans, and he'd huffed off. She wasn't entirely sure she'd have a job when she got back, but the event was too important to miss.

The party for Pops was supposed to be a surprise, so she didn't stop in Haven Shores to see him before continuing on to her bed and breakfast in Candle Beach. The party would be held at Sorensen Farm, an event center owned by Maggie Price, a friend of her brother's. Being in the same business, Zoe was curious to see how Maggie had renovated the old barn where the party would be held.

She caught a glimpse of Sorensen Farm as she drove around Bluebonnet Lake, but she wanted to keep her attention on the curvy road. Soon, she was driving down Main Street in Candle Beach. It reminded her a lot of Willa Bay with its cute shops, parks, and lack of stoplights.

The Beehive B&B was a few blocks from Main Street and looked like it had been an old motor court that had been remodeled in the last decade. Baskets of flowers hung from the eaves, with tendrils of red and white fuchsias dangling in the air. Zoe checked in and chatted with the owner for a few minutes, then decided to take a nap before dinner.

At half past five, Zoe woke from her nap and hurriedly got ready for dinner with Charlotte and Luke. She'd only met Charlotte once before, and she wanted to make a good impression.

She walked briskly to the Seaside Grill in the center of town and was escorted by a tall waitress to a table by the window. Luke and Charlotte were sitting together on one side of the table, and they stood to greet her as she approached them.

"Hey, sis." Luke pulled Zoe into an enthusiastic embrace.

"Hey." His chest muffled her words.

When he finally let her go, Charlotte smiled at her and gave her a light hug. "It's nice to see you again."

"It's nice to see you again too." Zoe grinned at her, then slid into the seat opposite them. "Thanks for planning Pops's birthday party. It feels weird not to be involved with such a big event, but I've been so busy at work as the wedding season ramps up."

Charlotte waved her hand in the air. "Don't even worry about it. Events at the Sorensen Farm practically run themselves."

Zoe raised an eyebrow. "That's impressive."

Luke laughed. "Charlotte may be exaggerating a bit, but Maggie does have a good system in place. I'm excited to see how everything turns out tomorrow night."

"Do you think Pops knows about it?" Zoe asked, sipping the glass of ice water the waitress had set in front of her.

He shook his head. "I don't think so. But I'm pretty sure his friend Joe would have spilled the beans if he'd had to keep the secret too much longer. Every time I visit Pops, Joe is just bursting to say something."

The waitress stopped by to see if they were ready to order, and Zoe realized she'd been so busy catching up that she hadn't looked at the menu yet. She scanned the entrées, but couldn't decide. There were too many good options.

"We're going to need a few minutes." Luke flashed a smile at the waitress, who nodded and walked away.

"Sorry," Zoe said. "I'll try to choose quickly."

"Uh-huh," Luke said. "When have you ever made a decision without fully investigating all of the options?"

Zoe rolled her eyes at him. "I'm not that bad." She closed her menu. "In fact, I'm going to get the salmon with roasted vegetables."

"Are you sure?" His eyes danced. "The shrimp scampi is excellent too, and I know how much you love shrimp."

Charlotte elbowed him in the ribs. "Stop teasing your sister."

Zoe shot Charlotte a grateful look. "Thank you."

"Yeah, no problem." Charlotte laughed. "I know how difficult he can be." She eyed Luke lovingly, and he kissed the top of her head.

"You have your moments too," he said.

The waitress returned, and they placed their orders.

When they were done and the waitress had gone, Luke fixed his eyes on Zoe. "So, how is everything going in Willa Bay?"

After the good-natured banter between the three of them, thinking about her job at the Lodge was like having a bucket of cold water dumped over her head. She stared at the table.

"Is something wrong?" Luke asked. "Are things okay at the Lodge?"

"Yes ... I mean, no." She sighed. "I thought I was going to be promoted to the events manager position when my current boss left this week, but instead, the Lodge's owner gave the job to his son-in-law, who's never worked in the industry a day in his life.

Charlotte's eyes widened. "Really? That's awful."

Luke pressed his lips together. "I'm sorry, Zoe. I know how much you wanted that job."

She shrugged. "Yeah, well, now I'm stuck in my current job for the foreseeable future."

"Are you thinking of trying to find something somewhere else?" Charlotte asked. "Maybe you could come back here?"

Luke's eyes lit up. "Pops and I would love for you to come back here."

"I don't know that Candle Beach or Haven Shores offer more options for event management jobs than Willa Bay," Zoe said. "They're all small towns."

"What if you started a business here?" Luke asked. "Maybe you could buy a renovated house and manage your own B&B or event space."

"Yeah," Charlotte said excitedly. "My brother and a friend of his have a business flipping houses in town. I bet they could find you something that would work. We could definitely use another B&B in Candle Beach. Even with the new hotel, we're still bursting at the seams during tourist season."

Zoe stared at them. Had they lost their minds? "This may shock you, but event planning doesn't pay big bucks. I'm fairly broke. Where would I get the money to buy a B&B in Candle Beach?"

Charlotte and Luke exchanged glances.

"If you need a silent partner, I'm your guy," Luke said.

"You'd invest in a business for me to run?" Zoe asked. "How can you afford that?" She knew he'd made good money while working at a San Francisco dot-com, but he'd bought a food truck he now ran in Candle Beach. Those weren't cheap to purchase or operate.

A wide smile spread across his face. "When I left the tech company I was with, I cashed in my stock options. After a few good investments, I have more than enough to live on. Heck, I could buy the Sorensen Farm twenty times over."

Zoe sat back in her chair, processing what he'd said. Pops had alluded to Luke having money, but it had never come up when she'd spoken with her brother, and she hadn't wanted to ask. Still, though, it made her queasy to think of borrowing money from anyone, let alone her brother. What if her business failed? She didn't want to let anyone down.

"Thank you for the offer, but I think I'm going to stay with my job at the Lodge for now."

He eyed her dubiously. "Okay, but I was serious. I'm always looking for good business investments, and I can't think of anyone I trust more than you to run an event planning business."

"I'll keep that in mind." She laughed, but her mood

was solemn. This conversation had turned serious all too rapidly. "How are things here in Candle Beach? How are the wedding plans going?"

"Everything's going according to plan." Charlotte's face glowed with happiness. "We've got the grounds at the hotel booked for the ceremony and then we'll have the reception at the Sorensen Farm."

"Is there anything I can do to help?" Zoe asked. It struck her as ironic that she was an event planner, and yet she wasn't around to help her own brother with his wedding.

"There is one thing." Luke's face was devoid of expression, and she wondered if something was bothering him.

"Anything." Zoe leaned forward in her seat.

A smile cracked his stolid demeanor. "Would you be my best man? Or rather, best woman?"

A thrill shot through her. "Really? Don't you want one of your friends to do it?"

He grinned. "I can't think of anyone I'd rather have standing up there with me on my big day. You've been with me through thick and thin, ever since we were kids. But don't worry, I'll have one of my buddies plan the bachelor party. You're off the hook on that one."

"Hey," Zoe said. "I *am* an event planner. I bet I could plan the best party ever – maybe a garden tour with afternoon tea. I know how much you love those little sandwiches."

A look of mock-terror came over his face. Next to him, Charlotte's mouth twitched as she attempted to keep from smiling.

"I'm joking!" Zoe laughed. "I'll make the sandwiches hearty."

He scowled at her. "I think I'd rather have Parker plan the bachelor party." He shook his head. "A garden tour ..."

"That may be for the best." Zoe winked at him, then turned to Charlotte. "Make sure to invite me for your bachelorette party though. I'd love to come up here early to help with it."

"I'll let Amelia know. She's taken on that responsibility." Charlotte sighed. "I can't believe it's only three months away. It seems like we've been planning it for ages."

"I know the feeling." Zoe smiled. Now they were speaking her language.

"Candle Beach could use a good wedding planner," Charlotte said. "I'm sure Maggie could use the help at the Sorensen Farm."

"Yeah, yeah, I get it. You want me to move here. You guys can quit the hard sell." Zoe laughed.

"She's onto us!" Luke said to Charlotte, who rolled her eyes at him in response.

Their food arrived, and they all tucked into their entrées, chatting in between bites. The way Luke looked at Charlotte made Zoe a little envious. They had such a strong connection, and she wondered if she'd ever feel that way about someone. She'd thought there might have been something between herself and Shawn, but he'd been somewhat distant since Celia woke up, so she wondered if she'd misread the situation.

After a long dinner followed by dessert, the three of them talked for a few minutes more on the sidewalk outside the restaurant. Zoe declined their offer of a nightcap at Charlotte's apartment. She was exhausted from the long drive from Willa Bay and wanted to make sure she was fresh for Pops's birthday party the next day.

"See you tomorrow." Zoe hugged both of them, then

walked down the side street to her B&B. She turned back one time and saw them walking with their arms around each other's waists, up the hill toward Charlotte's apartment over the bookstore.

～

The Sunday afternoon of Pops's party was sunny, and close to seventy degrees out. Zoe put on the white-and-pink flowered sundress that she'd bought for the occasion and brushed her dark hair until it shone. She assessed her reflection in the mirror and applied more blush to her pale cheeks. With Celia's hospitalization and everything going on at the Lodge, she'd lost too much weight, giving her face a gaunt appearance.

Luke and Charlotte's proposition for her to buy a B&B in Candle Beach may not have been the right move for her at this time, but for the sake of her health, she needed to make some decisions soon about her future at the Lodge. But this wasn't the time to dwell on her problems. This was a day to celebrate one of the most important men in her life and everything he'd done for her.

Zoe had about two hours to spare before the party, so she got in her car and drove out to the Candle Beach Hotel, which was a few miles out of town. She'd met one of the owners last year when he'd come to see the Willa Bay Lodge and she was eager to see what he'd done with the historic property. From what she'd heard, it had been in pretty bad shape when he'd taken on the project.

She parked in the gravel parking lot and walked along a path of white oyster shells until she stood in front of the hotel. It perched on a cliff overlooking the Pacific Ocean. The renovations didn't disappoint. It had been painted white and featured a wide, covered porch that wrapped around the building.

She continued walking along the path to get a better view of the exterior. Adirondack chairs had been placed along the back of the deck to take advantage of the expansive water view. Across the lawn, at the edge of the cliff, a gazebo – much like the one at the Inn at Willa Bay – watched over the grounds and the beach below. She backtracked along the path and climbed the short flight of stairs to the raised porch and entrance to the hotel.

Inside, a woman behind the front desk greeted her with a broad smile. "Hello. May I help you? Do you have a reservation for tonight?"

Zoe smiled back at her and moved closer to the desk. "No, I'm actually staying in town because you were completely booked for this weekend. But I met one of the hotel owners last spring, and I wanted to see how the renovations had turned out."

"Aidan or Amelia?" the woman asked.

"Aidan." Zoe looked around the room. "I actually work for the historic Willa Bay Lodge, north of Seattle, and Aidan and Maura came up to tour it to get some ideas for this hotel."

"Oh, that's so great that you were able to come and see it." The woman leaned forward giving Zoe the opportunity to see her name tag: *Tania*. "Actually, Aidan should be back soon if you want to take a quick tour."

Zoe checked her watch. There was still plenty of time to get to the Sorensen Farm before the party started. "Sure, that'd be great."

The woman lifted the phone receiver and spoke to someone, then set it down and turned to Zoe. "He'll be here in a few minutes."

Zoe nodded and looked around the room. An antique

loveseat sat under the window, its dark-blue fabric accented by the black-and-white floral tiles. Everything came together to give off the vibe of a comfortable, yet elegant lodging. "I love the decor."

"Oh, I know." Tania beamed. "Amelia, the other owner, is an interior decorator. She designed everything in here."

That explained it. Most designers took pride in their work, but this design was warmer and more personal than Zoe usually saw. If she ever had a place of her own, she'd definitely try to hire this interior decorator. Her thoughts came to a halt, and she stared into space. What was she thinking? Luke and Charlotte had gotten into her head with their talk of her owning a B&B or event space of her own. It was such a fantastical dream that it was laughable.

"Zoe." A man's voice broke through her trance. Aidan gave her a short hug and then stepped back. "It's good to see you! What brings you to Candle Beach?"

"It's Pops's eighty-fifth birthday party this afternoon." She gestured to the room with a sweep of her hand. "You've done a wonderful job with this place."

He puffed up a little. "It's all thanks to my sister, Amelia. Well, ninety-five percent of it is Amelia's doing. I handled the major structural projects, but she came up with the interior concepts." He peered at her. "How are things going in Willa Bay?"

She pasted on a fake smile. "Great! Wedding season is starting up, and we're almost completely booked out through the rest of the summer." She didn't want to get into everything going on at the Lodge. "So, Tania said you might be able to give me a tour? I'd love to see the place."

"Of course. I'd love to show you around. Let's start with the Great Room." Zoe followed Aidan into the large common space off the lobby, with doors leading out to the porch and magnificent views of the Pacific Ocean. He then showed her the rest of the interior, including a few guest rooms, followed by a quick tour of the grounds.

When they were standing on the porch in front of the lobby entrance, Zoe said, "Thank you so much. I really appreciate the tour and seeing everything you've accomplished here. Your success is well-earned."

He beamed. "Thank you." He nodded his chin at the door. "Maura will be here soon. I know she'd love to see you too. Did you want to join us for a cup of coffee?"

She shook her head. "I wish I could, but I need to leave for the party. I'm heading back to Willa Bay tomorrow morning, but next time I'm in Candle Beach, I'd love to hang out with you and Maura again."

"Sounds like a plan." He reached out to hug her. "Have fun at the party, and a safe trip home."

"Thank you, I will." She took one last look at the beautiful hotel, feeling slightly jealous of Aidan. "Have a nice night."

"See you later." He turned and walked into the lobby.

Zoe got back into her car and drove down the road to the Sorensen Farm. The party didn't officially start for another fifteen minutes, but the parking lot was already packed. Pops had a lot of friends. She parked at the end of a row, then walked into the freshly painted white barn.

Inside, hardwood floors shone with a recent waxing. Round tables that each seated eight had been set up around the edges, with a dance floor in the middle. Luke and Charlotte stood near a podium at the back of the barn talking to a woman with red hair. Zoe made her way to them through the crowd of people standing around in groups.

Charlotte grabbed her hand. "Maggie, this is Zoe. She's Luke's sister, and is an event planner up in Willa Bay."

Maggie smiled warmly at Zoe and held out her hand. "It's nice to meet you, Zoe. Luke talks about you often."

"Good things, I hope?" Zoe eyed her brother.

"Of course." He winked at Zoe. "We were just talking to Maggie about the order of things tonight. Pops is coming in about thirty minutes with one of his buddies. He thinks he's attending a wedding as his friend's plus-one."

Zoe rubbed her hands together with glee. "Ooh, I like it."

"I know!" Charlotte crowed. "I can't wait to see his face."

"As soon as Pops arrives, Maggie will come to the podium and announce that the party is in his honor." Luke wrapped his arm around Charlotte, who was still grinning from ear to ear.

"Okay." Zoe nodded. "Is there anything I need to do?"

"Not at first, but we'll need you to give a toast." Luke stopped and peered at her. "Is that a problem? I know how much you hated public speaking in school."

"Nope, I'm fine." Zoe laughed. "I got over that fear pretty quickly working in the event business."

"Well, it seems like we've got a great plan for the evening," Maggie said. "I think your grandfather is going to have the time of his life." She nodded at someone in the far corner. "I've got to take care of something, but be sure to flag me down if you need me. I'll be here all night." She smiled at Zoe. "It was so great meeting you."

"You too," Zoe said. When Maggie was out of earshot, Zoe asked Luke, "Does she attend all of the events here?" As the owner, Maggie would have other responsibilities too, and Zoe imagined it would be exhausting to attend every event at the farm.

"No, she wanted to be here for this one because we're

friends of hers," Luke said. "Plus, she lives in that farmhouse across the way, so it's not a long commute home. She's got an almost one-year-old baby girl and a nine-year-old boy, plus she owns a restaurant in town."

Zoe's jaw dropped. "Are you serious? How can one person do all that?" With the hours she herself worked, she was lucky to see her friends monthly outside of the Lodge. Having a family and a whole other business was out of the question.

Charlotte whispered, "I think she's the Energizer Bunny in disguise."

"No kidding," Zoe said.

The crowd hushed and turned in the direction of the door.

"Ned called and said they were about five minutes out," someone shouted. "Everyone, get ready!"

They all lined up near the door, waiting for Pops to arrive. Any latecomers were led around the back of the barn to enter from the rear door so as not to spoil the surprise. Zoe, Luke, and Charlotte made their way to the front of the crowd.

When Pops walked in, the barn erupted into cheers of *Surprise!* Pops looked around in confusion.

Maggie tapped on the microphone to get everyone's attention. "Our guest of honor has arrived. Luke, Zoe, do you want to show your grandfather to his table?"

"This is for me?" Pops asked Luke, who'd stealthily moved to his side. "I thought I was going to a wedding."

Luke nodded. "Yep. It's all for you. Happy birthday, Pops." He clapped Pops on the back. "And look who came all the way out here to celebrate with you." He turned Pops around until he was facing Zoe.

Pops's eyes were bright with tears. "Zoe." He wrapped his arms around her, hugging her tighter than usual and with more strength than she'd expect for an octogenarian.

His touch made her tear up as well. "Oh, Pops. I missed you so much." She was blubbering now, so happy to see him. She may have risked her job by coming out here for the party, but being here with her grandfather was absolutely worth it.

22

Meg

After a busy weekend at the Lodge's restaurant, Meg was happy to sleep in on Monday morning. She took a leisurely shower, then went grocery shopping and did laundry at her parents' house. Living alone in the studio apartment over their garage had its benefits – the rent was cheap, and having a small living space made housekeeping easy. She'd worried about living so close to her parents after being out on her own for so long, but with their opposite work schedules, she actually found herself wishing she had more time to spend with them.

Libby had invited her over for dinner and asked her to be there around five o'clock. Meg wasn't sure what to bring, so she set aside a loaf of fresh French bread, cut up some raw vegetables, and made a smoked salmon spread. She placed a bottle of wine in her tote bag for good measure. Libby hadn't been in the greatest mood lately, and wine might calm her down – or, at the very least, make Meg's evening better.

Libby and her husband, Gabe, lived in an old Cape Cod-style home that they'd renovated a few years ago to increase the square footage and accommodate their growing family. It was only a few blocks from where they'd grown up, in the same type of neighborhood filled with houses from the early 1900s.

As Meg approached the cement sidewalk to their front door, the sounds of screaming children emanated from the house. She rang the doorbell and waited on the postage stamp-sized front porch. From within the house, footsteps thundered toward her. The door burst open, and a little girl flung herself into Meg's arms, causing Meg to almost drop her tote bag.

"Hey, Kaya." Meg hugged her niece tightly and kissed her cheek, then looked past her. Where was Libby? "Does Mommy usually let you answer the door by yourself?"

Kaya shrugged. "No, but I knew you were coming to dinner." She tugged on Meg's hand. "C'mon."

"Who's at the door? Kaya? You didn't answer that did you?" Libby called out from the back of the house.

Kaya eyed Meg. "Oops."

"It's me," Meg shouted in the direction of Libby's voice. She and Kaya walked back to the kitchen where Libby was frantically loading the dishwasher. The kitchen was filled with the aroma of roasting meat and potatoes.

Libby fixed her eyes on her youngest daughter. "You know better than to answer the door without a grownup around."

Kaya stared at the floor. "But I knew it was Auntie Meg."

"You're still not allowed to answer the door unless Mommy has told you it's okay." Libby sighed. "Please go play with your brothers and sister now. And tell them dinner will be ready in about twenty minutes."

Kaya looked up at her mother, relieved to be out of trouble. "Okay, Mommy." She skipped away.

"Sorry," Meg said. She hadn't meant to get Kaya in trouble.

"It's not your fault," Libby grumbled. "She just doesn't listen."

Meg sat down at a barstool and watched as Libby stuck a detergent pod in the dishwasher and slammed it shut.

"Is there anything I can do?" Meg asked. She popped up from her chair. "Oh, I almost forgot. I brought some veggies and dip." She took everything from her bag and set them on the counter.

"Thanks," Libby said. "I already had veggies though." She put the dip on the kitchen table and moved everything else aside.

"Oh. Okay." Meg wasn't sure what she'd done to get on her sister's bad side or why she'd been invited for dinner in the first place. Libby hadn't exactly been friendly since Meg had moved back to Willa Bay.

Libby took an oval roasting pan out of the oven and lifted the lid, revealing a huge pot roast surrounded by baby carrots, potatoes, and onions in a rich broth. She added a bowl of button mushrooms into the mix, then replaced the lid and shoved the whole thing back into the oven.

"That smells wonderful," Meg said.

"I'm sure it's nothing compared to what you cook at the restaurant, but it suits us." Libby wiped the counter down, although Meg couldn't see any spills or crumbs on it.

"Pot roast is one of my favorite foods." Meg opened the bottle of wine and poured a glass, offering it to Libby.

Libby considered it for a moment, but declined. Meg

shrugged and kept the glass for herself. She watched as Libby pulled out a cutting board and bread knife, then sliced off a few pieces of the loaf Meg had brought, setting it on the kitchen table with the dip. While she worked, loud thumps from above shook the kitchen like there was a herd of elephants doing jumping jacks upstairs.

"Uh, is everything all right up there?" Meg asked.

Libby wiped the crumbs off the knife and stuck it back in its slot in the wooden block. Calmly, she walked into the hallway and shouted up the stairs, "Kids, knock it off. No more jumping off the bunk beds!"

Meg joined her in the hall. "They're jumping off the top bunk? Isn't that dangerous?"

Libby shrugged. "Probably. But if they get hurt, they'll learn. I've told them about a million times not to do it."

"Mommy," Libby's nine-year-old daughter, Beth, ran into the kitchen. "Tommy keeps stealing my pencils, and I need them to do my homework."

Libby sighed and opened a top drawer, withdrawing a handful of pencils. "Here. And try to go somewhere he's not around."

"He's always around," Beth whined. "He thinks that because he's in kindergarten now he can help me with my homework." She pouted. "He's so obnoxious."

"Okay, okay. I get it. Please tell him Mommy said he could play with his tablet." Libby leaned against the counter.

"Fine." Beth stalked out of the room.

Meg raised her eyebrows. "Is she always so dramatic?"

"Yep," Libby said. "Nine going on nineteen. I'm not looking forward to her teenage years." She filled her cup with coffee and stuck it in the microwave. When it beeped, she brought the cup to the table and sat across from Meg.

"I feel like I missed out on a lot of their childhood while I was living in Portland." Meg spread some of the pink salmon dip onto a slice of bread.

"You did miss out on a lot," Libby said tightly. She sipped her coffee and rubbed at a spot on the table with her index finger.

"What do you mean by that?" Meg tried to keep her tone level.

"Nothing." Libby stood and brought the raw vegetables over, then grabbed plates and cups to set the table.

She never stopped moving. Meg had always thought of her sister as Wonder Woman, getting twice as much done in the same amount of time as anyone else. But she hadn't considered how the stress of having so much to do affected Libby, let alone how she did it all.

"Are you doing okay?" Meg asked her older sister.

Libby flashed her a fake smile. "Of course. Everything's great."

Meg cocked her head to the side. "Are you sure?"

Libby's cell phone rang, and she answered it. After a few words back and forth with the caller, her face fell, and she hung up the phone.

"Who was that?" Meg asked.

"Gabe." Libby opened the refrigerator and pulled out the bottle of wine she'd stuck in there after Meg opened it. She filled a glass all the way to the top and came back to the kitchen table.

"Um ..." Meg stared at her. "What did he say?"

Libby gulped her wine. "He's not coming home for dinner tonight. He has to work late – again." The timer on the oven pinged, and Libby got up to take the pot roast out. She set it on a round trivet on the kitchen table, then went back into the hallway. "Kids!" she shouted. "Dinner!"

The herd galloped down the stairs, almost trampling their mother in the doorway.

"What's for dinner? I'm starved," eleven-year-old William said as he sat down at the table next to Meg. "Oh, hey, Aunt Meg."

"Hey, William." She grinned. She could still picture him when he was Kaya's age, prancing around on a stick pony. The years had gone by far too quickly.

The other kids sat down and waited while Libby carved the pot roast and dished up their food.

"I hate carrots!" Kaya complained.

"I don't really care," Libby said. "Eat them anyway."

"Where's Dad?" Beth asked. "He was supposed to help me with some science homework tonight."

"At work." Libby slapped a potato down on her own plate with enough force to rattle the glass dish against the table.

After Libby had finished getting her kids and herself food, Meg dug in. She took a bite of roast, savoring the herbs Libby had used to complement the beef. "This is really good."

"Thanks." Libby stabbed at her own meat with her fork and knife.

The kids ate rapidly, devouring their meals before Meg had eaten half of hers.

"I don't want to eat the carrots," Kaya said stubbornly. "I won't eat carrots. They're orange!"

Libby pushed back her chair and leaned her head in her hands. "Fine," she said through a curtain of hair. "Don't eat them."

"Really?" Kaya asked in an incredulous tone.

The other kids were staring at their mother knowing something wasn't right.

Meg stood. "Okay, kids, looks like you're done with

dinner, so you're all excused now. Go play or whatever you need to do before bedtime."

Her nieces and nephews looked at their mom, who didn't say anything.

Meg smiled at them reassuringly. "Go ahead. Your mom is just tired." In all honesty, that was probably part of Libby's problem, but there was definitely something else going wrong.

All four kids clattered out of the kitchen and up the stairs, leaving Meg alone with her sister, who hadn't moved.

Meg touched her shoulder. "Lib?"

Libby looked up, tears staining her cheeks. "I can't do this anymore."

Meg sat down next to her. "Do what?"

"Be everything to everyone." Libby sniffled and looked into Meg's eyes. "When Mom got sick, I was the one who took her to her chemotherapy appointments. Everyone else had to work, and they figured since I'm a stay-at-home mom, I have plenty of extra time." She sighed deeply. "Not that I minded being there for Mom."

"Is that why you're upset with me?" Meg leaned back in her chair searching Libby's face. "Because I wasn't here when Mom got sick?"

Libby nodded. "You were off in another state. You didn't have to see Mom hurting after her surgery or see how sick the drugs made her. Dad and Samantha helped as much as they could, but they both have full-time jobs."

Meg pressed her lips together. She hadn't known how much their mom's illness had affected Libby. Her sister was right though – Meg hadn't been there. She'd considered leaving her job in Portland immediately after finding out about her mom's illness, but she'd put off moving home for almost a year, at which point Debbie was almost done with chemo.

"I'm so sorry, Libby. I didn't know." She looked at the table, not meeting Libby's gaze. With it just being her, it wouldn't have been difficult to leave her life in Portland to move back to Willa Bay. "I probably should have come home earlier, but Mom kept telling me not to."

"I know she did," Libby said in monotone. "And you had a great job there that you'd worked hard for. You shouldn't have had to leave it. It's selfish of me to even say you should have. I just wish you could have been here to help with Mom. I can't do everything." Her face crumbled. "Gabe is never home, and I don't know where he is. He says he's at work, but I brought him dinner one night, and his car wasn't at the office."

"Oh, Libby." Meg hugged her close. She'd never seen Libby so undone. "I'm sure there's a good reason for him being gone so much. He loves you." Her brother-in-law had always seemed like a good guy who cherished his family, not someone who'd cheat. "And you are an amazing wife and mother. I seriously don't know how you do it all."

Libby took a shaky breath and dried her tears with a napkin she grabbed from the table, looking at Meg with gratitude. "Thank you. I'm sure the thing with Gabe is nothing. I'm just overly emotional from being alone with the kids so much and dealing with the stress of Mom's illness."

"I know." Meg smiled at her, feeling lighter than she had in weeks. Her sister's outburst had made everything in her life come into focus. "And you know what? I'm not going back to Portland."

Libby tilted her head to the side. "You're not? But I heard you got a job offer for some fancy restaurant there."

How had her sister heard about the job at La Lobessa? News traveled fast in a small town, and in her family particularly.

"Just an offer for an interview, but I'm not going to take it." Meg straightened her spine. "I want to be here to see my nieces and nephews grow up, and to be here for my friends and family – including you."

"But what about your career?" Libby reached for her wine.

Meg shrugged. "I have a good job right now, and I'm sure something else will come up in the future. I'm not worried about it."

"Okay." Libby gave her a tentative smile. "I'm glad you're staying. I've hated being upset with you, and I hope things can go back to the way they used to be."

"I'd like that." Meg stood. "Now, let's get this kitchen cleaned up before the little monsters come back wanting dessert."

Libby laughed. Together, they put away the leftovers and rinsed off the dishes, chatting rapid-fire like they used to when they were younger. By the time Meg left, Libby seemed fully recovered, but Meg knew her sister's fears about her husband lurked below the surface. Meg had always thought her sister was the one person in the world who didn't need anyone's help, but tonight's dinner had changed that perception. Meg intended to be there for Libby and the rest of her family and friends, whatever the future might bring. If staying in Willa Bay could achieve that, it was the right decision for her future, no matter how it affected her career.

23

Zoe

"It feels weird to be going through Celia's stuff," Meg whispered.

"I know." Zoe took a suitcase out of the closet in Celia's room and eyed the clothes hanging on the rod. What did her friend need while she was in the rehabilitation center? After Celia had woken up, Zoe had only spent enough time in her bedroom to grab a few things for her to wear. "What should we bring her?"

"Some shirts, and maybe some skirts or pants that will be loose over her leg?" Meg said. "Maybe a comfortable dress?"

Zoe grabbed everything that looked like it might work and brought them over to the bed, folding each item before placing it in the suitcase. "There." She looked around the room and picked up the framed photo of Charlie that sat on the nightstand. "I know she wanted this, but didn't she say something about a photo album?"

Meg nodded. "In the bottom drawer of her dresser."

She walked over to the tall five-drawer dresser and slid the bottom one out.

Zoe laid the framed photo in the suitcase and crossed the room to look in the drawer too. "That looks like a photo album." She pointed at a worn, brown leather book.

Meg took it out and opened it. "It looks like some really old photos of Celia with a young man. Maybe that's Artie?"

"Maybe." Zoe took the album from her to examine the photos. "It must be. Look at how they're staring at each other with so much love."

"Just the way you do with Shawn," Meg teased.

Zoe's face burned, but she didn't say anything. Although she'd eventually agreed with Shawn that Celia would need to move, things between them were still a little awkward. She flipped pages, stopping at a postcard of the Inn at Willa Bay that was printed on linen-style paper.

"It was so beautiful," Zoe said. It pained her to compare the Inn now to how it was pictured in the photo.

"Wow." Meg looked over shoulder. "Can you imagine what it was like to stay here back then?"

"I hope whoever buys this place decides to fix it up and not demolish it." Zoe's stomach twisted. Celia's property was one of the largest in the area, and with its view of the bay, it was likely to attract the attention of some big developers. All of the historic cottages and the main building at the Inn at Willa Bay could soon be nothing but a memory.

Meg rested her hand on Zoe's back and smiled at her sadly. "You never know. It could happen."

Zoe stood and took the photo album over to the bed, setting it in the suitcase on top of the clothes and the photo of Charlie. She pushed the lid of the suitcase down and zipped it, then lowered it to the floor. "That should be it. I'll take this over to Celia later today." She looked over at Meg. "Do you want some coffee? I think Shawn put a pot on before he left for the hardware store."

"Sure," Meg said.

They walked out to the kitchen together, with Zoe rolling the suitcase along the floor behind her. The coffee pot was still full, so they each took a cup out to the porch, where they sat in chairs overlooking the bay.

"I'm going to miss this." Zoe sipped her coffee and gazed out at the water. Gentle waves lapped at the shore, and the late afternoon rays of sun warmed the flowerbeds below the porch causing an intoxicating floral aroma to permeate the air. "I could seriously sit out here forever."

"Do you know where you're going to move to when the property goes on the market?" Meg kicked her feet up onto a footrest.

"Nope. I've thought about it a little, but with everything going on at work, I haven't made any decisions." Zoe leaned back in her chair and closed her eyes to allow the warm day and the rhythm of the waves lull her into relaxation.

"Any decisions about what?" Shawn asked from the lawn below them, a few feet away.

Zoe's eyes popped open and she sat up. "Shawn, you scared me."

Beside Zoe, Meg chuckled a little.

"Sorry, I didn't mean to startle you. You looked so peaceful up there." He joined them on the porch, pulling up a chair to sit nearby. "Man, it's days like this that I really wish I could afford to buy this place."

"I was just thinking the same thing," Zoe said wistfully.

"Maybe you *should* buy it," Shawn said.

Zoe laughed. "And maybe I should buy myself an island where I can do nothing but count my money all day." She looked over at him, expecting to see him smiling, but he wasn't laughing.

She sat up straight in her chair. "You're serious, aren't you? How could I possibly buy the Inn? Even if Celia accepted payments, I couldn't settle the tax debt before the county seizes the property, or afford the maintenance this place needs." Her words spilled out faster with each thought. "And what bank would loan me the money?"

"Didn't your brother offer to help you buy a business?" Shawn asked.

"Oh, yeah," Meg chimed in. "What about Luke?"

Zoe stared at each of them in turn. Were they crazy? They weren't talking about having her brother lend her a few hundred dollars. Celia's property was worth more like a few *million* dollars.

"I can't ask him for that much money," Zoe said. "It's too much." She'd made her own way in life so far, and she intended to continue that way.

"You'd pay it back once the Inn was up and running," Meg said. "Think of how popular the Lodge is. With all of the cottages here and the Inn itself, you could have triple the number of guests per night than the Lodge." She stood, spinning around to point to the far side of the house. "You could even have a small restaurant here, in the old barn. It has a great view of the water, and there's plenty of parking. With all the guests the Inn can accommodate, you'd have built-in customers."

Excitement swelled in Zoe's chest as she visualized everything Meg was saying. She could bring the Inn back to its former beauty. But was it too much to ask of Luke? From what he'd said to her when she'd seen him in Candle Beach, it wasn't beyond the realm of possibility for him to afford the property. Still, it was so much money to borrow from him with no guarantee she could ever pay it back.

Shawn reached forward to cover her hand with his, squeezing her fingers gently. "Zoe?"

"Yeah?" Her eyes met his, and the whole world seemed to disappear.

"I truly think you should consider buying the property. Think of what it would mean to Celia to see this place up and running again." He ran his thumb over the top of her hand as he spoke, sending tingles up her arm.

She forced herself to think clearly. She had to consider Celia. What would her landlord think of this whole crazy scheme? The Inn was all that Celia had left, but selling to Zoe had to be a better option than losing the property to a developer who'd tear the whole thing down and put up a bunch of cookie-cutter mini-mansions.

"Are you going to ask Luke if he'll help you buy it?" Meg's voice cut through Zoe's thoughts.

Zoe looked around, her excitement deflating as she remembered all the work it would take to renovate the property. She was used to planning events, so managing a big project didn't scare her, but still …

"I'll ask," she said. "But on two conditions." She grinned at them.

Meg cocked her head to the side. "What are they?"

Zoe looked at Shawn, then Meg. "That Shawn will help with the renovations and that both of you will come on as my business partners. And maybe Cassie too."

Shawn nodded. "I'm up for it. I'd love to make this place shine again, and I'd love to do this for my grandmother."

Meg eyed her with skepticism. "I'm a chef. What do I know about running an inn?"

"Remember that restaurant you said would do well here?" Zoe asked. "Well, I'm going to hold you to that. As soon as we can get the main guesthouse fixed up, we can start on turning the barn into the nicest restaurant in all of Willa Bay." She eyed Meg. "Provided, of course, that I can get Luke to invest in the property in the first place."

Meg's face lit up. "My own restaurant? Here in Willa Bay?" She scooted forward on her chair. "We could be like Suki and Lorelai on Gilmore Girls, running an inn and restaurant together. Do you really think we can do this?"

Zoe took a deep breath. "I don't see why not. I'm going to give my brother a call to see if it's even a possibility. If he gives us the green light, all of us can head over to the rehabilitation center to talk to Celia.

To gain some privacy while she spoke with Luke, Zoe walked over to the stairs down to the beach. She dialed her brother and held the phone to her ear as she descended, admiring the work that Shawn had put into the steps and railings. Given a chance, he would do an excellent job of renovating the Inn.

Her heart hammered harder in her chest with every ring. Finally, after about five rings, Luke answered.

"Hey, Zoe, what's up?" People jabbered in the background and she had a hard time hearing him.

"Are you at work?" Despite being a closet millionaire and having employees to help run the BBQ food truck he owned in Candle Beach, he often worked there himself.

"Yeah, why? Can you hear me okay?"

"Not really. I can call back later." She hated to put off asking him, but she didn't want to bother him either.

"It's fine. Give me a minute." The noise levels decreased, and his voice came over the line again. "Is this better? I walked down the block a bit."

"Yes, thank you." She paused. Asking her brother for

something this big was one of the most difficult things she'd ever done in her life. She knew he was happy to help her, but she still didn't like the idea of needing his help. "I have an investment proposition for you."

"Really? What is it?" His voice rang with surprise, likely because she didn't usually ask him for anything.

"You know the cottage where I live, right?" she asked. Luke had visited her in Willa Bay a few times over the years and stayed at her house.

"Right. What about it?"

"Well, I'm not sure how much of the property you saw when you were here, but it used to be part of an old inn that was popular back in the early to mid-1900s."

"I remember seeing a couple other small houses there and the big place where your landlord lives," Luke said. She pictured him pacing along the sidewalk below the lot where he parked his food truck.

Zoe pushed forward. "I didn't tell you when I was in Candle Beach, but my landlord had an accident and is now in a rehabilitation center to get physical therapy for her hip. She's fine," she added hurriedly, "but the property isn't. When she was in the hospital, I learned that she hasn't paid taxes on it for years, and the county will seize it soon for back taxes."

"So, you want me to help her pay her taxes?" Luke asked. "If that's what you need, I can do it."

"No." She breathed in the salt air, letting it fill her lungs and refresh her courage. "I'd like to buy the property and restore it back to how it used to be." Even though she knew he couldn't see her, she swept her hand out in front of her as she spun around in a circle to see the bay, the inn, and a glimpse of the cottages through the trees. "Willa Bay is growing, and I think with a proper renovation, we could have a successful resort and restaurant here. I haven't talked to my landlord yet about it, but I think she'd agree to sell to me."

"Okay. You want me to buy the Inn." Luke was quiet for a moment.

Zoe tried to wait out his pause, but she couldn't stop herself from blurting out, "I know this is a huge investment, and if you can't afford it, I totally understand. But you'd offered to help me start a business, and I just thought I'd ask—"

"Zoe, stop," Luke said. "I did say I'd help you, and I meant it. I'm not worried about how much it costs. I'm sure I can swing the purchase price and fund the renovations. I trust you. If you say it's a good investment, I'm sure it is. But it sounds like you need to work out some of the details with the current owner. Why don't you discuss it with her and then we can go from there? Once you've agreed on a purchase price, I'll have my real estate attorney draw up the paperwork. Does that sound good?"

It sounded better than good. Zoe was floating on air at the thought of saving the Inn. "Yes. I'll talk to her today. But there's something else – I'd like to bring in a few of my friends as business partners, if you don't mind."

"I think that sounds like a wonderful idea." Luke's voice warmed. "And, sis, I'm really glad you called me. I feel like we haven't spent enough time together in the last few years."

"I know," Zoe said. "I've been thinking about that a lot lately."

"Would it be okay if Charlotte and I come up to visit you on Thursday?" he asked. "I know you have work, but maybe we could meet you for dinner?"

"I'd love that." Zoe grinned. "I'm off at five, so let's meet at my cottage around five fifteen, and I can show you around your new investment."

He chuckled. "I look forward to seeing it."

"I'll see you on Thursday. Thank you again."

"See you then."

The call ended, and Zoe hung back by the edge of the cliff for a moment, taking it all in.

This beautiful location could be hers. The feeling was heady, and she wanted to share it with Shawn and Meg. She ran across the lawn to the porch, where they were eagerly waiting to find out how her discussion with Luke had gone.

"He said yes!" she shouted. "Let's go talk to Celia."

Meg and Shawn looked at her, wide-eyed, then both sat back in their chairs, probably experiencing that same life-changing feeling she'd had.

Meg stood from her chair. "I'll go get her suitcase."

She went inside, and Shawn walked down the front steps to meet Zoe on the lawn. He reached out and captured Zoe around her waist, pulling her close to him. Her heart beat double-time as she looked into his eyes. He bent down and tentatively touched his lips to hers. She leaned into him, snaking her hands around his neck. Sensing her approval, he deepened the kiss. She closed her eyes, letting the dizzying sensation of being close to him sweep over her and blend enticingly with her excitement about the Inn. After a while, he broke the kiss, but continued to hold her against him.

"I take it you're not upset with me anymore?" he asked.

She shook her head. "I'm sorry I got so angry with you. I wanted Celia to be able to come home, and I didn't want to accept that it wouldn't work out."

He laughed and tenderly brushed a stray wisp of hair away from her face. "Well, it turns out that you may have been right. If I make the main house more accessible, what do you think about having Celia continue to live in her own bedroom? We'll be around all the time in case she needs help, and she'll love interacting with the guests once we open the Inn to the public."

Zoe stared at him in wonder. "I hadn't thought about it yet, but that's a great idea." She gave him a quick peck on the lips. "I can't wait to tell Celia."

Meg clambered down the steps, holding the suitcase. "I'm so excited. I can't believe this might actually happen."

Shawn held his key-ring up in the air. "I'm ready if you are." He grabbed the suitcase from Meg and set it in the trunk of his car.

As he got into the driver's seat, Meg whispered to Zoe, "Are you two together now? I saw you kissing."

"I hope so." Zoe's heart soared, thinking about the kiss she'd shared with Shawn. When she'd first talked to him, she'd never have guessed how much she would grow to care for him. Seeing his kindness toward Celia, a woman he'd never met before, had endeared him to her in a way she hadn't expected.

"It's about time." Meg hopped into the back of the car, leaving the front passenger seat for Zoe.

Zoe climbed in and looked over at Shawn. He smiled at her, leaned over and kissed her lightly on the lips, then turned the key in the ignition. Zoe relaxed against the leather seat and let her thoughts drift to the future as they headed down Willa Bay Drive to see Celia.

24

CELIA

Celia sat in the dining room of the rehabilitation facility with Cassie, drinking coffee and eating donuts.

"These are good, but next time I visit you, I'm going to bring you some of the coffee cake I make at the Lodge," Cassie said. "I know how much you like it."

"Thanks, I'd love that." Celia smiled. She did love coffee cake and ate at least one piece of it every time Cassie brought it to church for refreshment time. She observed her young friend. Cassie had been through a lot in the last few years, with her divorce and all of the challenges of being a single parent with young children. Through it all, Cassie had maintained her customary positive attitude – but something seemed different now.

"Can I get you some more coffee?" Cassie touched the handle on Celia's cup.

"Oh no, dear. I'll be floating if I have any more." Celia finished the last bite of her powdered-sugar donut and daintily dabbed at her mouth. "How are you doing? How is work? And the kids?"

Cassie sighed and looked into her coffee cup. "Work's been better. With Lara back in town, George has decided that it's not a good idea for me to make the cakes for my side business in the Lodge's kitchen."

"Oh no." Celia leaned forward. She'd never been a big fan of the Camden family. "What are you going to do?"

Cassie smiled softly. "Luckily, Debbie has kindly offered to let me use her catering kitchen, but that's only temporary. I'm hoping to be out of there in a few weeks, so I don't intrude on their space for too long."

"Are you going to find another kitchen to rent? Or start your own bakery?" Celia asked.

"I'm not sure." Cassie sighed. "I hadn't really given much thought to opening my own bakery, but I guess it's something I could consider in the future. It costs so much money and time to start, though, and I'm strapped for both as it is."

Celia nodded her head slowly. "That's understandable. You've got a lot on your plate."

Excited voices entered the cafeteria, and Celia turned around to see who'd arrived. Zoe, Shawn, and Meg were approaching her table, all of them grinning from ear to ear. And were Shawn and Zoe holding hands?

Celia smiled as they neared. "Hello. Did you come to join Cassie and me for some coffee and cookies?"

"We might do that," Zoe said. "But we came to talk to you. The three of us have a proposition."

"Oh? What is that?" Celia asked. From the anticipatory looks on their faces, she had a feeling she already knew.

"You know none of us want you to have to move from the Inn, right?" Shawn asked.

"Uh-huh." Celia watched them keenly, interested to hear their plan.

"Well, the three of us came up with an idea of sorts." Zoe spoke animatedly. "We'd like to buy the Inn property from you and renovate it. With how much Willa Bay is growing, I think it could be a hugely successful resort and event center. My brother is willing to loan us the money to buy it from you at fair market value."

Shawn took a seat next to Celia. "The best part is that you could stay in your current bedroom and be the Inn's host." He looked up at Zoe. "Of course, we'd be there to help with managing the place, but you could make guests feel at home when they arrive."

Meg turned to Cassie, who'd been watching them intently, her expression a mixture of joy and sadness. "Cassie, we'd love for you to join us, if you're interested."

Cassie smiled. "Thank you for thinking of me. Celia and I were just talking about what I can do in the future, but I don't think owning an inn is the best fit for me."

"Oh." Zoe's smile sagged. "It would be so much fun to do this together. Think of all we could do with it."

Shawn searched Celia's face. "What do you think?"

"Hmm ..." Celia's pulse quickened. How would they take her response? She loved all of them and didn't want to disappoint them. "I'm going to have to turn down your offer."

Shawn sighed. "But if you don't come up with the tax money by next month, the county is going to sell the house out from under you." He ran his fingers over the top of his hair, a gesture that reminded her so much of Artie. "We don't want to force you to sell the Inn to us, but this seemed like a good option. With Zoe's project management skills, Meg's restaurant knowledge, and my love of craftsmanship, we could make it viable again."

Celia decided to not leave them hanging. She grinned widely. "I know all that. That's why I talked to my lawyer about selling half of my interest in the Inn to you all, and putting the other half of it into a trust with a life estate. When I die, the trust will be disbursed to your partnership and Shawn's sister, Jessa." Celia eyed each of them in turn. "If you're still interested, I'll call my lawyer and tell her to draw up the papers."

"Wait." Zoe's tone was incredulous. "You'd thought about all of this already?"

Celia chuckled. "I started thinking about it as soon as I woke up from my accident. I realized I needed to start relying on my friends and family a little more." She grinned. "I may be old, but I'm not senile. I think you'll make a wonderful management team for the Inn, and I'm happy to stay on as the official welcome wagon for guests."

Meg nudged Zoe. "And we thought we were so smart, huh?"

Zoe laughed and met Celia's gaze. "I'm sorry if I underestimated you. I should have known better. But are you sure you want to gift it to us?" She rested her hand on Shawn's arm. "Shouldn't Shawn and his sister inherit the property in full?"

Celia looked fondly at Shawn. "I'm excited to share what time I have left with Shawn and Jessa – if she'll have me – but you girls have been my family for as long as I can remember. I know you'll take care of the Inn for me."

Zoe, Meg, and Shawn looked at each other and nodded in agreement.

"I think we're going to take you up on your offer." Shawn leaned over and hugged her, filling Celia's heart with happiness. It had been so long since she'd allowed herself to hope for a future with Andrea's family, that it seemed like a miracle to have it come true.

"I think this calls for a group hug," Cassie said. "I'm looking forward to seeing what you all can accomplish at the Inn."

They all gathered in near Celia and embraced her. The other patients and staff at the rehabilitation center stared at them, but Celia didn't give a fig what they thought. The people surrounding her with their love were her reason for getting up in the morning – and now she knew for sure they would be there for her in the future, whatever it may bring.

~

Zoe

"This place is beautiful," Charlotte exclaimed as she stepped out of the car onto the lawn of the Inn at Willa Bay. "I can't wait to see what it looks like once you've renovated it."

Zoe smiled. "I know. I'm looking forward to seeing it too." She assessed the property with the eye of someone who'd never been there before. The buildings weren't in great condition, but it wasn't hard to imagine them at their finest, with guests playing croquet on the lawn or enjoying a cup of tea on the porch. She eyed Luke anxiously as he exited the car. "What do you think?"

He scanned the house and grounds, then locked eyes with Zoe. "I think you've got your work cut out for you, but if anyone can make this place shine again, it's you." He shaded his eyes with his hand. "Is that a gazebo over there? Hey, Charlotte, want to come check out the view?"

Charlotte nodded. "I want to see everything." She sighed. "I'd love to paint the Inn while I'm here. With the varying blues of the sky and bay, and all that green grass, the colors are breathtaking."

"We'll make sure to leave time for you to paint." Luke reached his hand out to Charlotte. She twined her fingers through his, beaming as she continued viewing the grounds. "Zoe, we'll be back in a bit. I just want to see a few things first."

"No problem. Dinner should be ready in about thirty minutes." Zoe turned and went up the steps to the porch.

Inside, Shawn was wrapping bacon around some asparagus. He lifted his head and peered around her. "Are they here?"

"Yep. They wanted to see the exterior of the Inn before dinner." She took the lid off of a pot on the stove, releasing a cloud of steam and the scent of boiled potatoes into the air. They broke apart when poked with a fork, so she turned off the burner and drained the water from the pot. With a hand mixer, she blended them into a creamy mash with a splash of milk and a hefty portion of butter.

"Did Luke seem to like it?" Shawn asked. His voice held a tinge of concern.

Zoe chose her words carefully. "He thinks it's a big job. Charlotte was impressed though." Her future sister-in-law's exuberance for life and positive outlook was good for Luke. He'd always been very serious, even as a child, and Charlotte was exactly what he needed to gain some balance in his life. "Luke's not going to back out on the deal though. You don't need to worry. He already gave his word, and he's not one to renege on a commitment."

"Good." Shawn came up behind her and wrapped his arms around her waist. "I like him already."

Zoe smiled, but it felt like pinballs were ricocheting off

of her insides. This would be the first time Luke had met one of her post-high school boyfriends, and she didn't have a clue how he'd react to Shawn. "To tell you the truth, I'm a little nervous about the two of you meeting."

"It'll be fine," Shawn whispered into her hair as he lightly kissed the top of her head. "I'm a great guy. Everyone always likes me." He stepped back and winked at her to let her know he was joking. "But in all seriousness, I'll be on my best behavior."

Zoe stood on her tiptoes and kissed his lips. "You'd better be."

"Hello?" Luke's voice came from the front door. "Can we come in?"

"Be there in a minute," Zoe called out. She set the mixer by the sink and rinsed off her hands, drying them on a dish towel. "I guess this is it," she said to Shawn before heading to the front door.

Charlotte and Luke stood on the porch together. Charlotte was still looking around, taking in every detail of the grounds.

"Come in, come in." Zoe gestured to the living room off the entry hall. "Have a seat. Dinner's almost ready, but I'll go grab Shawn so you can meet him."

"Good." Luke's voice was gruff. "I hope he's as wonderful as you claim."

Heat rose in Zoe's cheeks, and Charlotte elbowed Luke in the side. "Luke! Be nice!" she hissed.

"Yeah, yeah." Luke sat down on the couch with Charlotte next to him.

Zoe retreated to the hallway and steeled herself with another deep breath. Luke had always been critical of her boyfriends in high school, so she'd considered not telling him anything about her new relationship with Shawn. She and Luke didn't see each other often, though, and she wanted to start her future off with full honesty. Besides, at some point, Luke had to approve of one of her beaus.

Shawn had just removed the roasted chicken from the oven when she reached the kitchen. She hung back for a moment, watching as he checked it with a meat thermometer, then slid it onto the plate. She loved watching him work – seeing the obvious care that he put into everything he did, from carpentry to cooking.

"Dinner's ready," he announced with a smile.

"Do you have a few minutes to come meet Luke and Charlotte before we eat?" she asked.

"Of course." He washed his hands and dried them thoroughly. "Let's do this." He followed her back down the hallway to the living room.

"Hi, I'm Shawn." He stretched out his hand to Luke.

Luke looked him up and down, then rose to his feet and shook his hand. "I'm Luke. Nice to meet you."

"And I'm Charlotte." Charlotte shook Shawn's hand as well. "Are you the one who's responsible for the flowerbeds outside the house? They're lovely."

"Thank you," he grinned. "I've been working on them for a few weeks. Some of the flowering shrubs are original, but I've planted some annuals, as well, for color."

They chatted for a few minutes, then Shawn invited them into the dining room, where he and Zoe served dinner. During dinner, the conversation flowed freely, and the tension gradually dissolved from Zoe's neck and shoulders. Shawn was relaying a tale about the house he'd renovated, and Luke was listening intently. Zoe bit her lip to control her relief. Her brother actually liked one of her boyfriends.

When they'd finished eating, Zoe pushed her chair back and gathered everyone's plates into a pile.

"That was delicious." Luke laughed good-naturedly as

he leaned back in his chair. "I'm guessing it was Shawn who cooked tonight? I'm not sure my sister can make toast, let alone a big chicken dinner." He looked at Zoe. "Remember when you were in high school and wanted to make an egg salad? You left the eggs on the burner so long that the water all boiled off and the eggs started melting onto the pot. I didn't even know that was possible."

"Haha," Zoe retorted. "I'll have you know, my skills in the kitchen have come a long way since we were kids. I made the potatoes you ate three helpings of." She eyed him smugly, then smirked. "But Shawn did make the rest of the dinner."

"Well, thank you for the excellent meal, Shawn," Luke said. "How did you learn to cook like that?"

Shawn shrugged. "I've been an Army bachelor for most of my life. If I didn't make my own food, I had to eat in the mess hall. Anything I made had to be better than the slop in some of those places." He took a long sip of water.

"Would anyone be interested in a walk down to the beach?" Charlotte asked. "The sun should be setting soon, and I'd like to get some reference photos so I can paint a picture of the Inn at sunset when I get home."

"I'd love that," Zoe said. "Let me clear the table and then we can go." She picked up two of the water glasses.

"We'll help." Charlotte handed Luke the stack of dirty plates and grabbed the empty mashed potato and asparagus bowls.

Shawn picked up the large oval platter he'd served the chicken on and carried it into the kitchen, leaving only the cups on the table for Zoe to get. They made short work of storing everything away, then put on their coats and went outside. With the sun down, the temperature had dropped into the low fifties.

"I don't know why, but it always surprises me how fast it gets cold when the sun goes down." Zoe stuck her hands in her pockets and shivered.

Shawn wrapped his arm around her waist and pulled her close to keep her warm. They all made their way down to the beach, stopping to sit on the log Zoe had sat on a few weeks before. The sun sank lower on the horizon until it disappeared below the surface, painting the sky with streaks of pink and violet.

Charlotte snapped photos in quick succession. "I'm going to head down the beach for a few minutes to see if I can get a picture of the cottages in the last bit of light." She jumped up from the log and walked along the sand, and Luke jogged after her.

When they were alone, Zoe turned to Shawn. "This wasn't too bad, right?"

He smiled softly at her. "I think it's going well. Your brother and Charlotte seem like good people."

"They are." Zoe glanced at Luke and Charlotte, who'd stopped down by the water to photograph some seagulls wading in the shallows.

Shawn looked over at them, then gazed into Zoe's eyes. "You know, I'm really glad I met you. It may not have been under the best of circumstances, but I couldn't have asked for a better outcome."

"Me too." She smiled up at him.

He turned slightly on the log to face her, caressing her cheek with one hand while wrapping his other arm around her waist, then kissed her sweetly on the lips. She leaned into it, resting her hand on his back. A light breeze rippled the air around them, but she was warm and content being there with him.

When the kiss ended, she kept her arm around him and nestled her head against his shoulder. From here, she had a clear view of the gazebo high up on the bank above them, the fading white paint glowing in the light of the moon. A contented smile spread across her face. Maybe there was a chance for her dream wedding in the gazebo, after all.

EPILOGUE

Cassie sat on a beach log and gazed up at the Inn at Willa Bay. It was Memorial Day weekend, and renovations were in full swing. Zoe, Shawn, and Meg planned to open the Inn for reservations by the end of August.

While Meg had opted to stay in her job until they were ready to take on the huge project of turning the old barn into a restaurant, Zoe had happily bid farewell to her position at the Lodge. She and Shawn were currently clearing away blackberry bushes that were encroaching upon the trail that ran along the embankment above the beach.

They were working side by side tearing out the prickly vines, and obviously enjoying each other's company. Cassie watched as Shawn struck an amusing pose with the rake, and Zoe stood on her tiptoes to kiss him, the sound of her joyous laughter floating all the way down to the beach.

Cassie grinned. After meeting Shawn, Zoe seemed to

have changed. She'd always been career-driven, but he'd helped her to achieve some balance in her life. Now, she was happier than Cassie had ever seen her.

"Cassie?" Kyle said.

Cassie turned to face him. "Is Jace done taking pictures of the island?"

For Jace's tenth birthday, he'd requested a small family picnic at the beach instead of a big party. He'd always had a special interest in sea life, so when he'd suggested a picnic at the beach, Cassie had been all for it. Since the local parks would be jammed with people over the holiday weekend, Zoe had offered Cassie the use of the Inn's beach and grounds. Although the tidelands technically couldn't be divided into private property, the Inn was at least a mile away from the Willa Bay Beach Park, and people seldom ventured out that far.

Kyle nodded. "He and Amanda want to explore some of the tide pools, so I was going to head down the beach with them to that big rock that's usually half underwater. Do you want to come with us?"

Cassie stood and brushed the sand off her pants. "Sure."

Jace and Amanda had already taken off at full speed in the direction of the large black boulder, but Cassie and Kyle followed at a more leisurely pace.

"I don't think I've ever seen the tide this low," Kyle said.

"Me neither." Most of the boulder that normally peeked just above the waves was visible, and the kids were already clambering around it. It was good to see Jace enjoying something other than Legos or video games.

"What did you find?" Kyle called out as they neared the big rock.

"I found a jellyfish," Amanda shouted with glee. "Come see it!"

Cassie and Kyle dutifully trotted over to see the creature, then stepped back to allow the kids room to continue their exploration.

"How are things going at work now?" Kyle asked. "You haven't said anything about it for a while."

Cassie eyed her ex-husband. It was like he'd turned over a new leaf in the last few months and become a more considerate, courteous version of his old self. Or maybe they'd just reached a point in their divorce where they could be friends again. Whatever it was, it was nice to be on better terms with him.

"About the same. Lara's still making messes, and I can't say anything to George about them." She sighed. "I miss having Zoe there, and Meg's counting down the months until she can quit. Everything's different."

"What about your side business?" Kyle asked. "Maybe you could do that full time?"

She snorted. "Unless I find a space of my own, I'm pretty much at capacity. I can't use Debbie's catering kitchen forever because they're taking on more jobs now. Besides, what would I do for health insurance?"

"I'm sure you could figure something out." He stuffed his hands in the pockets of his jacket and looked into her eyes. "If you could do anything for a career, what would you do?"

She didn't hesitate. "I'd own a bakery." After Celia had brought up the possibility last month of Cassie opening her own bakery, Cassie hadn't stopped thinking about it. She'd even gone so far as to make an appointment at the local Small Business Administration office, but she'd chickened out and canceled it.

"Then you should do that." Kyle searched her face. "If that's your dream, you should go after it."

"But where would I get the money for it? Starting a business isn't cheap." She looked out at the water, her thoughts spinning in her head like the waves swirling around the boulder.

"I've got a little money saved up," Kyle said. "I'd be willing to invest in your bakery."

Cassie stared at him. Seriously, who was this guy? She shook her head. If she was going to do this, she needed to do it on her own. Their divorce had taught her that she needed to stand on her own two feet and not always be dependent on someone else, even if they meant well.

She smiled at him. "I appreciate the offer, but I'd like to look into some other options first." She straightened her spine. "I'm going to go down to the Small Business Administration office this week to talk to them."

Kyle nodded his head slowly, then gave her a small smile. "I think that sounds like a good plan."

"Dad." Jace came over and tugged at Kyle's arm. "Come see the sea star! One of its arms is shorter than the other."

Cassie and Kyle followed him over to a pool of water in a large crevice in the rock. Sure enough, a red sea star clung to the rough surface.

Cassie crouched low to see it closer. "It's beautiful." Jace had been correct – one of the arms was about half the size of the others. "I wonder what happened to it?"

"I'm sure it can't be an easy life for them out there." Kyle turned to Jace. "Did you know that sea stars can regenerate their arms? It can take a year or more, but they'll eventually grow a full-size limb."

"They sound like pretty resilient creatures," Cassie

said. "It's cool that even when bad things happen to them, they just keep going and eventually overcome it."

Jace stopped and stared off into the distance for a moment, then looked over at his parents. "Kind of like you, Mom. Your life is really different than it used to be, but you always keep going." His face lit up. "Hey! If you open a bakery, you should name it the Sea Star Bakery." At that, he walked away to inspect the other side of the boulder.

Cassie and Kyle looked at each other.

"Did he hear our whole conversation?" Kyle asked. "I didn't think he was listening. He was so intent on checking out the tidepools."

She laughed. "His hearing is amazing when he wants it to be." She sobered. "I hope he didn't hear too much though. I don't want the kids to worry about us having enough money, or about my job."

"I'm sure it's fine," Kyle said. "I wouldn't be too concerned about it." His attention turned to Amanda. "I'm going to make sure she doesn't go out any further, or she's going to swamp her rainboots."

He walked over to where Amanda was wading in the shallow water, and Cassie moved closer to Jace. Her son was a constant mystery to her. One moment he could be distant, then loving the next. His comparison of her to a sea star had come out of the blue, but it was an astute observation. She rolled the name around on her tongue. *Sea Star Bakery*. It did have a nice ring to it.

Kyle, Amanda, and Jace were now looking at something together. Cassie thought about joining them, but decided not to. Even though she and Kyle weren't together anymore, it was still nice to see him interacting with the kids and for the four of them to spend time together as a family.

The last two months had been so full of changes, both in her own life and those of her friends. Cassie had never expected to see workaholic Zoe quit her job at the Lodge, but her friend seemed deliriously happy now, both with her decision to buy the Inn at Willa Bay and with her newfound romance with Shawn. And though Cassie had secretly hoped Meg would stay in town, it still surprised her that Meg would give up her dream to be a chef in a big city.

Like it or not, life was full of changes, both good and bad. Cassie glanced back at her kids and ex-husband. As the tide swirled higher around the boulder, she knew the tidepool exploration portion of their day would soon be over, but she resolved to enjoy whatever came next in her life. No matter what the future may bring, she would always be there to support her family and friends.

~

Thank you for reading The Inn at Willa Bay! I hope you enjoyed reading the first book in the Willa Bay series as much as I did writing it. If you're able to, I'd love it if you left a review for it.

Wondering what's in store for Cassie? Find out what happens next with Book 2, The Sea Star Bakery.

If you haven't read the Candle Beach series, check out Book 1, Sweet Beginnings.

Happy reading!

ACKNOWLEDGMENTS

Thank you to everyone who's helped me with this book, including:

Editors: LaVerne Clark, Devon Steele

Cover Design: Elizabeth Mackey Design

Made in the USA
Middletown, DE
24 September 2023